# SAINT LUCY

Jesse VanDeWalker

ISBN 978-0-9885373-0-9

*Dedicated to the days we built
these paper mountains.*

*Let's sit and watch them burn.*

# PROLOGUE

They had already blocked most of the windows off with furniture and doors, but a few on the second floor were still open, allowing Corsey to get a look at what was going on in the front yard. A rope was hanging from the old tree out there, and the lynch mob didn't look to be breaking up anytime soon. He let the curtain fall back into place and turned around to face the woman behind him.

"How does it look John?" Her dark hair was done up in a bun and she wore a simple dress with an apron tied around her waist. The rifle she held at port arms didn't match anything she was wearing, aside from the look in her eyes.

"Like something we can handle. I'm going to want you on this window." She nodded and checked the chamber of her rifle for a cartridge.

"I'll watch the window. Where will you be?" He pulled his revolver and checked the chamber, giving it a quick spin before snapping it back into place with a flick of his wrist.

"Using up some of these shells."

# ONE

The desert sun beat down hot, and Corsey walked back to the little hacienda he and Lydia had found. It had been just where Reed had written them it would be. He stood in the doorway and watched her sweep the dirt floor of the little hut with a straw broom until she looked up, meeting his eyes.

"He's three days late. If he doesn't show by dusk, we ride on in the morning." He was using a neutral tone, testing the waters. She smiled at him and replied,

"Well, if we had a better, or even another, job lined up, I'd agree. On the other hand, we've food for another week, and we haven't heard a word from Jones or any other law since Crow Wing. I say we stay for at least that long." She said, pretending to concentrate of sweeping. He crossed his arms and thought for a moment before speaking,

"Just because we haven't seen any law doesn't mean Jones isn't tracking us, and especially you. Two days."

A few months back, Marshal Harvey Jones had formed a posse to chase the stage robbing gang outside Crow Wing, California. Lydia had hidden the gold from the stage inside her traveling trunk until Corsey had been able to come and get her from Sacramento. Lydia had gotten a twinkle in her eye while John was woolgathering.

"Four more days at least. We've got to do something, and this is all we've got." She had stopped pretending to sweep.

Corsey kept his arms crossed and gave her a hard look. "Less expensive if we hadn't armed every rogue native band we come across, besides putting them in steel tools and blankets. Three more." he said.

Now it was her turn to give him a hard look. "I didn't question you on how your share was spent. Three days it is. Now, if we're done arguing over how much longer we wait why don't we

7

go over what the 'southern gentleman' is trying to say in this mealy-mouthed letter?"

Corsey nodded and uncrossed his arms, walked to the table at the center of the single room and picked up the letter, reading it over again.

They had spent two months on the move letting Jones sniff after cold trail until heading to Shorty's Hotel in Clear Water, Colorado to pick up Corsey's mail. In that bundle of letters had been only one which contained an offer on a job that hadn't expired. That one offer came from Josiah Reed, lately of Georgia and read as such:

*To one Mister Albert Fisk,*

*I have heard of a service you once rendered a friend of mine in Kentucky, he recommended you to me and allowed that I should write to you at Shorty's Hotel in Clear Water, Colorado.*

*I am certain you could help me with a situation that has recently vexed me concerning the ownership of*

8

*a certain item. Your expertise would be highly valued and surely helpful in resolving this matter.*

*If you can spare the time, meet me outside High Springs, Alachua County in New Mexico Territory. I suggest a date three months from the date of my mailing of this letter, I know that in your business, travel is often necessary and so I will allow a margin of error in the case that you don't receive this letter in a timely manner.*

*I have additionally included a map of the area around High Springs and the location where I will expect you.*

*Please be sure to lay in supplies for yourself as I am unsure what kind of welcome I will be able to offer you.*

*Your servant,*
*Josiah Reed*

Corsey went under the Fisk name when he was in Clear Water to keep any law or anyone else off him in one place of the world at least, but it had been three days since Reed had said he would be at the meet. Lydia watched him expectantly and he handed the paper over to her. She read it more quickly than him and paused for a moment to gather her thoughts.

"This bit about Kentucky was a job you pulled. He wants you to steal something for him, but he doesn't mention how much he'll pay." She parsed the details out loud.

"Yes on both. Not mentioning a price makes him for new to hiring thieves. The rest of the details should only be face to face, letters can be opened by anyone, which makes him for cautious at least." he elaborated. He didn't add that putting in the spot of the actual meet was a little amateurish.

She waited for him to go on, and when he didn't she asked, "He shouldn't have said where he's meeting you. Will he set a price, you think?" She still held the letter, nearly forgotten in one hand.

He stood quiet, his hands in his pockets. "If he doesn't, we don't work. Some amateurs will want to promise you part of the future sale of the stolen goods, but the better way is to negotiate a price before the job, and get half up front and half after the work is done." He seemed to be on the verge of saying more, but stopped and looked to her, waiting.

"So it's best to get half the money up front... because otherwise a double cross is too tempting?" She went on, answering her own question, "Of course it is, to get your goods for the cost of a few bullets and a bit of blood instead of currency. But how can you know the hiring party won't still cross you?" She asked the question, even though she was fair certain she knew the answer.

He shook his head and took off his hat. "You can't."

# TWO

Marshal Jones had been following the cold trail of Lydia Driscoll for three months. By now he knew that she was traveling with an unidentified man. The Marshal also knew he was far, far behind her. Too far to catch up without some kind of luck, and the only luck Jones had had with this chase had been bad.

First, his former deputy-turned-sheriff and an entire posse of men killed by the stage robbing gang that Jones suspected Lydia of being part of. Second, she disappears right out from under his nose in Sacramento. Last, the only leads he had dried up before he ever came across them.

Jones figured this was on the part of the mystery man Lydia had attached herself to. Men in that line who lasted any amount of time often proved wilier than an old fox. This man, whoever he was, seemed to be no exception.

## Saint Lucy

The Marshal trailed them from California across the Rockies, and then north for a time. Somewhere after the fourth week he lost the trail completely until he stumbled across a barkeep who recollected a near fatality in his establishment not one full moon past. concerning the virtue of a white girl wearing a traditional red man type outfit. Jones knew it could only be Lydia, and set out in the direction the bar man had indicated they had ridden.

It had led to whole mess of nothing once again. Not being the kind of man to enjoy being frustrated, Jones decided to try to identify the mystery man Lydia was traveling alongside, since tracking her led to nothing, nothing and more nothing. Jones rode for Sacramento to start over.

He spent a week looking in Sacramento before deciding there wasn't anything to find, and went back further, to Crow Wing. The only thing he was apt to find there was Daniel Washburn, who was dead from a slit throat on a dusty road. The rest of the Marshal's leads were drier than the dirt Daniel had bled his last on.

The new Sheriff wasn't half what Jerry Brooks would've been, he didn't know the people, the sore spots, the men to watch. Jones had known that before he got there and he didn't look to the Sheriff for information. It took the Marshal a week to track down the hunters and trackers that had survived riding out with him in the posse that had looked for the stage robbers, but it paid off in the end like he had hoped it would.

He asked them all the same questions: How many men do you figure pulled that job? Which direction did the survivors ride after the showdown at the bog shack? Had they noticed any strange campfires or groups moving around in the few weeks after the robbery? Nearly all the men had answered in the negative. Nearly.

The Marshal picked through the ravaged remains of a substantial store of food and water at a tiny shack in the middle of nowhere: the perfect place for a hideout after a stage robbery. He found several discarded scraps of burlap, most with the once bright red and now faded to pink stamp of a trader; a trader's mark he recognized.

Jones knew the man operated a post a fair bit north of Crow Wing, and east of Sacramento. Combined with the sewn-together burlap he had found where the stage was robbed, Jones had the first real pieces to the puzzle he had been trying to assemble since the long, long day when Washburn and eleven other men had died.

The trading post hadn't burned or been abandoned.

The Marshal rode up on the post, not really looking at the place. It was like a hundred others he had seen, and a hundred others he would see. He swung out of the saddle and tied his horse at the rail, listening to the trader hustle out to meet him.

"Howdy sir," the trader greeted him, "Water and feed your horse?" The trader already had the grain scoop in his hand. Jones nodded, replying,

"Yeah. This is rough country hereabouts. I'm surprised you ain't been burnt out by outlaws or Indians. Yet." Jones let that sink in before he went on, "Yeah, I imagine most of your trade is with the local tribes. Had reports in Sacramento that tribal violence is on the rise. Better armed than usual, I guess."

Jones squatted briefly to get the stiffness out of his legs as he spoke. Though he couldn't see it, he imagined the look on the face of the trader to be suspicious. The Marshal turned to face the man, showing the trader the star on his chest. "You got any firearms in there? Ammunition? If you'd fill my feed bag, and answer a few questions, I'd be obliged."

Mentioning the penalty for arming renegade natives and supplying them with ammunition were reason enough for the trader whose mark Jones had found at the unused hide to remember what the man who had purchased such an odd amount of

16

burlap looked like. Jones carefully took notes while the trader described the man who had made the exchange, a man Jones had never heard of before. He was on the right track.

After the trading post, the Marshal traveled east for a time, looking to dig up some information on the identity of the man who had visited the post.

# THREE

"He's got until dusk." After three full days, Corsey was ready to move on, job or no job.

Lydia set her hands on her hips and looked ready to start a new war between the states.

Corsey cocked his head to one side and held a finger to his lips. "One horse and rider, coming from the southeast. Get ready." He ducked inside to grab his gun belt off the table.

Lydia grabbed her rifle and checked the chamber before moving out of the door after Corsey. She positioned herself to cover the southeast as he walked slowly out, one hand resting lightly on his right hip, ready to pull the pistol that hung heavy there.

They both watched the rising dust cloud shimmer in the midday heat as the rider drew closer. She watched as John tipped his hat back and wiped his brow, keeping the sweat out of his eyes. Lydia spared a glance for the vegetation, it was yellow and stunted, but grew nonetheless. She briefly thought, *How stubborn a plant must be to survive in all this desert.* The sounds of the approaching rider drew her attention back to aiming her rifle and keeping her sight lines clear.

John stood where he had stopped, unmoving after wiping his brow. Waiting to find out if the rider was friend, foe or client. The rider was nearly upon them, and she took careful aim at his main body mass. He was there, in front of John and she strained to hear what the newcomer was saying while also keeping him covered.

"Mistuh Fisk, Ah presume?" The man was undoubtedly a southern dandy, judging by the way he dressed, rode and spoke. His dismount was a pretty thing to see, all flourishes and swinging legs, Corsey could have shot him four times during the ridiculous-looking exercise. He wore a fine white suit, now creased with trail dust and stained with sweat; it fit him well and he looked well fed but not fat. His face held that haughty look only the old money South could manage when they looked upon their lessors.

Corsey had spent enough time in the south to hear past the man's drawl and quickly got used to it. He crossed his arms and stayed out of Lydia's line of fire.

"You're late." he said.

The other man, presumably Josiah Reed, took off his hat and fanned his face dramatically. "This surely is hot country. Georgia gets hot, but this is an entirely different order of heat. Where are my manners?" The dandy extended his right hand towards Corsey. "Josiah Reed, Mister Fisk, a true pleasure to meet you."

John let him hang his hand out there for a moment. "You can call me John, you can put away that hand and you can tell me why you're late before I ride on." Corsey had not moved.

Reed looked put out as he withdrew his hand and continued to fan his face with his hat. "We could surely discuss these matters once seated in the shade of the shelter I have provided, couldn't we, John?" Reed asked. Corsey uncrossed his arms and started walking to the small outbuilding that his and Lydia's horses were stabled in. "Wait, Mister Fisk, I can explain! I was unavoidably detained by those damned-ably persistent Texas Rangers!"

Corsey stopped walking and turned slowly around, right hand close to his gun and his eyes scanning the scrubby country surrounding the little house. "Last chance Reed. Explain yourself and tell me you weren't followed, or I ride on after I shoot you for a fool."

Reed's composure and time had almost run out. Lydia could tell, and not just from his shouted comments about the Texas Rangers. She sighted once again down the barrel and waited for gunfire or parlay.

She had looked around slowly when John dropped his right hand to his hip and started scanning the brush, but she hadn't seen or heard anything out of the ordinary. One reason John had put her on this duty was that her woodcraft was better than his, and he knew it. She would have heard or seen an ambush coming long before he would have in this wild country.

He was better at knowing when to expect an ambush, something she was still learning. Reed was saying something, she couldn't make it out through the drawl and the distance. Now tossing his arms wide, showing exasperation or surrender.

John was saying something back, too low to make out but he looked more relaxed and he wasn't looking all around for possible Ranger ambushers.

"I was not followed, and that is precisely why I am lamentably late! Please sir, let us not come to gunfire, who have just met to discuss most profitable business! Now can we please retire to yonder hovel and talk business?" Reed said.

Corsey relaxed his posture, giving Lydia good body language for *'don't shoot the dandy'*.

He waved Reed to the door ahead of him. "You're going to have to explain why the Rangers took an interest in you. Sit down here." Corsey slid the chair out that sat facing the wall opposite the door and then walked around to sit facing the doorway. "Sit."

Reed sat and made a show of fanning his face energetically and smacking his lips.

"There'll be water after you explain yourself, Reed. Get to it."

The face that the dandy had worn up until that point slipped for a split second. Though the glare that he shot Corsey could have left scorch marks on the table, John didn't move a muscle, but he did take notice.

Reed's face quickly resettled itself back into the mask he seemed more comfortable wearing. "Very well, if common table manners don't apply, we should proceed into business. I need you to steal something for me, something beyond the measure of price."

Reed waited several seconds for Corsey to reply, and when John only sat and waited in turn Reed continued.

"The item is a painting, left in this country by the conquistadors over two hundred years ago when the French seized the Spanish holdings here in the New World. It depicts the holy Saint Lucy who plucked her eyes from their very sockets when a pagan boy complained of being tormented by the beauty of them.

Her eyes were soon restored to her during prayer at the chapel, and the young man was so impressed by the strength of her faith that he immediately converted. Not long after the pagan authorities heard of her activities and arranged for her to be given into the service of a brothel.

She would not be moved however, and so they put her to the torch. Not even the flames could touch her and so they slew her with a sword, thrust into her neck.

The artist was Zubarán, a disciplined 1500's Spaniard."

Corsey sat through Reed's talking; not needing the information about the history of the painting, but knowing that if he tried to rush the man all he would get is more time wasted. He sat and listened to the maybe-dandy roll out all the unnecessary facts until Reed got to the point.

"The painting is inside a stately manse located in the Saint James Parish in Louisiana, called Constancia. It is surrounded by what was a sugar plantation, recently run to riot by poor upkeep and mismanagement. I know little enough of the interior or habits of the residents of the manor house, but I suspect that acquiring such information would be your very stock-in-trade Mister Fisk. Unless I misjudge you, of course!"

Reed sat back in his chair waiting for Corsey to respond, but the other man just sat. Sat and stared across the table, his eyes flat and unreadable to Reed.

Finally the man Reed had called 'Mister Fisk' spoke. "Why?" He didn't normally care about who wanted what stolen and why, the how of it concerned him wholly enough, but there had been that one slip of the mask from the dandy when proper etiquette had not been followed, and Corsey wanted to hear more about this particular job before he signed on.

Outside, Lydia sat and listened.

"Ah'm delighted you asked, Mistuh Fisk! Ah've told you a good bit about the paintin's history but left out one veruh important fact. Reputedly, behind that painting, in the frame, lies a map to conquistadoh gold, seized from the savages in Mexico and taken to Louisiana. Apparently those intrepid Spanish explorehs trusted theih gov'mint to take care of them roughly as much as we here in the south trust ow-us to take care of ow-uh interests up there in Washinton!" Reed was trying what John had predicted.

Offering a piece of the profits from the recovered item was a real greenhorn idea. Lydia crept close to the hacienda after the two men had walked inside and listened to the visitor talk about the job. His accent grated on her, it seemed that he couldn't speak more than one sentence for every breath.

John said little however, so she knew he was interested. How he could sit and listen to the man's ridiculous accent, she didn't know. He did, and so she did as well.

# FOUR

Josiah sat at the table without his water and continued rattling off the history of the painting located in Constancia. The item was in the second floor study, a room co-opted by his grandmother years before his birth after his grandfather had died of tuberculosis. He told Fisk none of the family history, feigning ignorance about the plantation entire. He could tell that the man he had come so far to hire had as little interest in the how and why of the painting as Josiah himself had ever had, but he sawed on anyway, keeping his cover intact. While he let his mouth run, his mind drifted back to just why the Rangers had pursued him, and to what and how much he was going to tell Mister Fisk about that encounter.

In the morning he had ridden out and left the angry eyes of the madame behind him without a care, but by midday he would have a reason to care what she thought of him.

He heard the first hoof beats far behind when the wind suddenly dropped off. A quick look behind him showed a dust cloud rising from a single rider who was clearly riding his backtrail.

He snorted, thinking of the previous night's entertainments with the sow. No doubt she had some fool cowpoke chasing after him with delusions of reclaiming her honor. She had been pretty in that common way, after all. The trail had been running parallel to some washed out gullies, but they wouldn't provide much cover. The rest of the land was mostly flat, with some little roll to it.

Instead of trying to hide, he reined in and turned, waiting for the fool behind him to catch up. In the meantime he checked his revolver, a seven shot pistol, inlaid with silver filigree and handles of carved ivory. He lifted his hat and looked up briefly, checking the more important of his two weapons.

Reed looked at the man who

had spent the better part of two hours catching up to him. His horse stood taller at the shoulder than the rider. No doubt the little gnome was afflicted with some type of Napoleonic disorder, creating in him a need to prove himself the better of any man who topped him in height. Presently, the pugnacious imp made his position clear.

"You Reed?" the small man asked.

Josiah nodded slowly, waiting for what came next.

"I'm Anders, Texas Rangers."

Josiah felt his right eye twitch in surprise, but it was too late to run and hide. The man being law did make killing him out of hand a bit more problematic, but Josiah weighed the pros and cons carefully as he waited for the Ranger to go on.

"Figure you know why I been following you. You might be something back in Alabama or Georgia or where ever the hell you come from, but here folks answer for what they done." The law man waited for a reaction, most likely a vehement denial, from Josiah.

Josiah continued to weigh his options. The sun inched closer to the western horizon while the two men sat and looked at each other.

Anders spoke again, "I'll have to ask you to surrender any weapons you might be carrying, and to submit to me tying your hands until such time as we can go before a judge and settle this." The Ranger was already reaching for his lariat.

Reed again nodded slowly and opened the right side of his coat, carefully removing his showy pistol from its holster and handing it to Anders.

"Well. Anders, was it?" Reed asked. While the Ranger was unloading the pistol and nodding in answer to Josiah's question, Josiah took off his hat and looked skyward. He reached into it as he noted the Ranger's gaze following his upward. He continued, "It was good to meet you, Texas Ranger Anders." The two shots from the hidden derringer in Josiah's hat turned the quizzical expression that had just begun to form on the face of the Ranger into a bloody mess.

Josiah slipped the small gun back into its hiding place in his hat before clapping the hat back on his head and swinging a leg over his horse to dismount. He bent at the waist and pulled a knife from a hidden sheath in his right boot. He stepped forward, went to one knee and cut the law man's throat.

He retrieved his gun, reloading it slowly while he thought out his next move. No doubt others would follow young Ranger Anders when he didn't return with the big bad man in tow. A quick double shot echoed back over the hills making Josiah hunch his shoulders protectively. He hadn't counted on the Ranger having back up so close to hand. Josiah, not knowing the proper counter sign to say all clear, swung back up into his saddle and rode hard north, hoping to cross into Indian Territory before the rest of the Rangers caught up with him.

The time it had taken to shake the Rangers had made Josiah late for the meeting and almost blew his chance at getting a man as qualified as Mr. Fisk in on his scheme. He was nearly finished with his prepared speech on the history of the painting and why he wanted it stolen so very badly. It was time to decide what to tell the man about the Rangers.

# FIVE

It took Marshal Harvey Jones some time to sniff out the back trail of the mystery man, which meant the crook must have been mostly small time before taking down the stage outside Crow Wing and killing a whole mess of deputies and law men. Jones stopped in every one horse town on the way to Kansas.

The Marshal made his way slowly across that state, until riding into a town called Durington, in Beecham county. A trio of wanted posters caught his eye there. Two he recognized as dead men, and the third matched the description of his mystery man, who now had a name: Richard Roberts.

Taking the wanted poster with him, Jones mounted up for the long ride back west, mentally mapping the route he would take. He would have to be careful to hit all the out-of-the-way hidey holes that outlaws like Roberts would want to frequent while keeping from the long arm of the law.

Jones rode a rancher's holdings in northern Wyoming for a few days, scouring the low foothills for bandit camps. The rancher himself had been nothing but obliging, offering the hospitality of the bunkhouse, if the Marshal was of a mind. More often than not, the Marshal was. The rancher himself wasn't often in evidence, preferring the seclusion of his big house to the rowdy company of his men.

One afternoon Jones figured he had looked hard enough, so he knocked on the door of the big house.

"What can I do for you, Marshal?" The rancher answered quickly, greeting Jones warmly.

"Figure I've put upon you long enough, sir. I'll be heading on in the morning. I don't mean to impose, but do you think we might have a cup of coffee?" Jones replied. The rancher nodded and ushered Jones to a seat in a small drawing room. The man hustled out to make the coffee and Jones looked around. It was only the second time he had been inside the house, and the first time he had been in this room. It was a nice place, not too fancy, but still nice. The rancher didn't have a servant either; just like his house, he was nice, but not too fancy.

"You take sugar or milk, Marshal?" the rancher called out from the nearby kitchen.

"No thank you, I'm sorry to say I've gotten used to drinking it black after being on the trail for so damn long." Jones listened to the rancher shuffling around in the kitchen and drew his pistol, laying it on the table. From his jacket, the Marshal pulled a scrap of burlap. A reply called out from the kitchen,

"Black it is then. Sorry I can't offer you something to chew on, but I normally take my meals later in the evening." the rancher came back into the room, bearing two tin coffee cups. His eyes went immediately to the burlap, and only after to the gun. "I make a mean cup of coffee Marshal, but you won't have to shoot it first, I assure you."

"Sorry about that, Mr. Sunshine. I get a might twitchy when someone as handy with a gun as yourself gets out of my sight for any amount of time." Jones took the offered cup of coffee and rested it on the arm of his chair. "Sit down."

Roberts failing to deny that he was Richard 'Sunshine' Roberts was a dead giveaway, but Jones had mostly thrown it out there to assuage his own conscience that he was dealing with the right man. Roberts took his seat across the table from the Marshal. The thin robber-turned-rancher set his cup aside and his shoulders slumped as if under some great weight. His head hung low, Roberts spoke, "What do you want, Marshal?"

Jones sipped his coffee.

"Start with Crow Wing, California and go on from there." U.S. Marshal Jones had found his man.

# SIX

Corsey could practically see the gears turning behind eyes of the southerner as the other man droned on about the origins of the painting; Reed was clearly thinking of something else and doing a poor job of hiding it.

There was a problem with that. If he didn't care about the story of this painting, why was he going through the motions of pretending that he did? There was something in this Reed didn't want Corsey looking too closely at, so Josiah was spilling out a load of fool's gold to get his attention. The real question was whether or not Corsey should look as if he was buying into it, or as if he couldn't care less one way or the other.

Safer to play it the second way. He wasn't much of an actor. He could see the dandy was starting to wind down about the manure neither one of them cared about, so he spoke up.

"This isn't the kind of

information I need to do this job. I need to know more about where the painting is, what kind of guards it has, who's going to miss it and why the Texas Rangers would spend the better part of a week chasing you through the brush and Indian Country before we can talk about anything else."

Reed didn't miss a beat.

"Well, as to the Rangers: It seems they had an issue with my refusing to allow a fellow poker enthusiast an extra hole card up his sleeve."

Reed was smooth, and believable. Corsey waited for more. Rangers wouldn't have followed Reed over a dead card sharp.

"It turns out that the cheater was a ne'er-do-well cousin or some such to one of those fabulous Rangers. He of course, had trouble swallowing that I shot his beloved cos over a palmed ace of spades and so came at me. I was forced to defend myself, not knowing what a hornet's nest I'd be kicking over at the time."

When it was clear that Reed was

done spinning straw into gold, Corsey sat forward and clasped his hands together on the table in front of him.

"So you're telling me you killed two men, one of them a Texas Ranger and the other a cousin to the dead Ranger." Corsey thought about the whole picture for a moment, wondering if it was worth trying to sort out the truth from the bullshit.

At least part of what Reed was saying was true, but there was something else. If the part he was lying about was the dead cardsharp, why lie about killing a man who cheats at cards, but admit to killing an officer of the law straight out?

Corsey shrugged his shoulders and shook his head, showing Reed he didn't believe the lie, but also didn't care. Corsey leaned back and brought over the water pitcher and cups from the sideboard.

"All right. Now we can talk about the painting."

Reed smiled widely.

Outside the window, Lydia settled in. She carefully did not make any noise, and listened to Reed talk. Though his accent and mannerisms grated hard on her, she tried to shake that off and judge the truth in his words. He was lying.

John clearly didn't believe him either, but apparently decided it didn't matter all that much. Still, something about the southerner entire stuck sideways in her craw. She had a feeling that whatever he was leaving out, lying about, was a bigger deal than John seemed to think. She heard the water in the pitcher slosh as it was moved to the table and poured. The sun was still beating down hot but she sat and waited all the same. John could need her at a moment's notice.

"As I said before, John, I know little of the inhabitants of the manor house or how well guarded the painting is. I don't believe the owners are aware of the hidden map, or they would be much richer than they are. As far as possible competition, the only other man that knew about the map told me with his dying breath where it lay.

"I do know that the painting is treasured by the family that holds it, and they will immediately note its absence from the house. Best you be far away when that happens, I think." Reed paused and grinned.

Corsey sat and listened, rolling his cup back and forth in his hands as his mind worked.

"The grounds around Constancia are well maintained by a loyal cadre of servants, but the sugar fields are completely overgrown and nearly impossible to navigate. If you can get me the painting whole so that I can remove the map myself, and also authenticate it, I will pay you a sum of three thousand dollars." Reed waited for Corsey's reply and it came quicker than he expected.

"Eight, and half up front. This information you're giving me won't get me inside the house. Hell, it won't get me within shouting distance of the house without getting caught. I need to know what size the painting is, can one man move it? Will I need to put together a string of men to get me in and out with the painting? These are questions that need to be answered, and if I have to go get the information myself, I expect to be paid for my time, understand?"

Reed's smile withered at Corsey's relentless tone. "Eight thousand dollars! I could buy the damn painting for eight thousand dollars!"

Corsey shook his head and put his cup down. "This isn't a negotiation, I'm not selling you a goat or melon here, Reed. I'm a professional quoting a price for a service to be rendered. You can either agree or find another professional. And, if you could buy the damn painting, we wouldn't be sitting here."

Reed sat back, astonished. "Well, I did not anticipate such a savvy haggler as you seem to be when I wrote you, Mr. Fisk. I thought there would be some room for give and take on the price of this service. However, if eight thousand will guarantee me my map, it is a small price to pay."

Corsey continued, "Four up front and four when you have the painting. I assume you don't have the money here, so we'll need to set a drop where you can leave the first four for me." He watched Reed carefully. It was all a little too easy.

"You are correct in assuming I don't have the four thousand here, but are you sure about just 'dropping' four thousand dollars American? How do I know someone else won't get to it before you? Then you don't do the job, and I'm out the four?"

Corsey sat back, ready to explain all the details of the drop with patience.

He and Lydia had work.

# SEVEN

The coffee had long since gone cold and taken on the consistency of mud, but Jones had gotten what he had come for. Roberts hadn't wanted to talk, but some busted ribs and a couple of mashed-up fingers later, Jones had the whole sorry tale. The Marshal had suspected that there were more men in the job then the dead Daniel Washburn and the previously unidentified two corpses. Jones now knew them to be Big Ben Overton and Fat Joe Collins.

He thought that Roberts might be the final piece of his puzzle, but Lydia Driscoll queered the whole thing for him. She wasn't with Roberts and her body hadn't turned up, so where did she finish after the disappearing act in San Francisco?

Now Jones knew: Lydia was with a man named John Corsey, who could be found fairly regularly at a joint called Shorty's in Nederland, Colorado.

Jones was still reviewing all his new information as he swung up into the saddle. He turned his horse's head east, and gently tapped the big animal's sides with his boots. As he settled into the rhythm of riding his hands shook, but only a little.

The coffee was lukewarm, and Richard Roberts was still talking about the set up for the job that had gone down in Crow Wing earlier that year. Jones had already figured most of that for himself. He was gauging Sunshine's ability to lie. So far, he hadn't, at least that Jones could tell.

"So we decided to ambush the wagon from the rear after we had it stopped short, and the whole plan came from John from there." Roberts' voice was dry, and tired-sounding. He could have been reciting a bill of sale or a dental procedure for all the involvement he had in the telling.

For that reason, Jones was watching him like a hawk, noting every movement, every hesitation. Lying to the Marshal wasn't going to be easy.

Roberts paused to catch his breath, and order his thoughts. He was going to have only one chance to lie, so he knew he'd better make it a good one.

"What you're telling me, Roberts, is that you just gave the money to an unknown, untried, slip of a girl on the say-so of this Corsey? No offense, but I find that a bit hard to swallow. I mean to say, it seemed to work out for you well enough, what with the little house and the land and the string of horses." Jones sat back, scratching his stubbly jaw. "Aw hell, it did work out! Go on then, what else?"

Roberts sat quietly with his hands folded neatly in front of him and raised one eyebrow slowly. "That's all there is to it, Marshal. You know the rest about chasing us and Big Ben getting his and Joey crawling off to die somewhere. We, meaning John, Lydia and I, met back up and split the earnings.

"I come out here to make an honest living, and then you show up on my stoop. I haven't heard a whisper of Corsey nor young Miss Driscoll since we parted ways at that campfire, right after the split." Roberts stopped himself; he was still in known territory. So far he was telling the truth to this very dangerous Marshal, and didn't want to use his one chance to lie just yet.

The Marshal was waiting for Roberts to go on. He had obviously stopped mid-stream. Jones leaned forward, his chair creaking comfortably underneath him.

"Come along now, Sunshine. You weren't through yet. Sure, you had big plans to go straight, and why not with your whole gang dead? Smart fellas like you, you've always got an extra escape route planned, just in case. Fellas like you think everything through twice, and you musta had the thought that this little equine venture just may not work out, so tell me."

Roberts shook his head and leaned back in his chair with a deep sigh. "I don't know what you mean, Marshal."

Jones' tone stayed friendly, and his face kept smiling, but his body language was telling all kinds of stories about how people get hurt when they lie. "You do know what I mean and you do know how to get hold of John Corsey. Just in case. Now you're going to tell me how to get hold of him, just in case something happens to you before I get you to a jail cell."

Jones' grip on the butt of his pistol tightened a bit as he prepared mentally, in case Roberts decided to go for some last ditch weapon.

What Roberts actually did came as more of surprise than if he had yanked a howitzer out from behind his back.

# EIGHT

Lydia was seated across from Corsey at the small table, the dandy having long since ridden back east to Alabama. The night outside the window—where she had spent most of the afternoon sitting--was humming with insects, but the girl had ears only for the job. The light inside the *hacienda* came from a greasy old oil lamp, and it cast flickering shadows over John's face. Normally by this time at night they'd have made love and been asleep in the narrow cot in the corner, but tonight they were making something else. She listened intently as he spoke.

"We need to know the layout of the inside of that house. The only way I'm getting in for a look is under cover of night, with the risk of ruining the whole job. On the other hand, Reed's hiding something. That something could come out to bite us right in the middle of this thing, or it could be nothing."

She looked at him minutely. "But you don't think so."

"But I don't think so." He was about to speak again, but he could see that far off look in her eyes that meant she was working it all out on her own. More than her womanly charms or her no-nonsense demeanor, he loved her for that look.

"You want me to get a look at the house without arousing suspicion." She wasn't asking, so he let her go on. "I suppose I could go in as a prospective buyer or a lover of southern antiquity... but then I'd only get one look. To get next to the house, I'll have to get next to the people in it. That means a maid or a cook or some such."

He began to speak, but she didn't look at him as she rolled out the rest of her thought process.

"Meanwhile, you'll be casting around looking for anything Reed might not have told us." A slow smile started at the corners of her mouth. "I don't know which of us will have the worst lot out of this John, you with the swamp rats and pond scum, or me with the once high-and-mighty southern aristocracy!"

Corsey didn't smile. "I'm not going to tell you to do this Lydia. It'll be dangerous, especially since we don't know what Reed is hiding. We could hire a pair of eyes just as easy as send you in there." He didn't say 'alone.'

Lydia had proven, time and again, that she was more formidable than most *men* on the wrong side of the law.

She shook her head, her black hair tumbling a bit into her eyes. "No, John. Remember when I said we were to be equals? This is what I meant. We both have to run risks, or we're not equals. Besides, you wouldn't trust anyone else to bring you an accurate floor plan of the inside of this Constancia, just like you wouldn't trust anyone else to dig up whatever there is to find on Reed."

He nodded slowly, looking out the window.

Lydia, after sitting and listening

to the two men talk earlier in the day, remembered something that had struck her as odd. "He lied. Not about killing a Ranger, but about why he had to. He was too proud of that to be lying. It seems not a little strange to me that he would lie about one but not the other. That may be a good place to start trying to find out just what he's hiding."

Lydia was mostly talking to herself, but Corsey was inwardly surprised. He had picked up on the lie, but figured the man had just been caught doing something embarrassing. She was right however, the best place to start back-trailing Reed would be in whatever mess he had stepped in just before coming to the meet. Now she was looking out the window, thinking with that look on her face that he loved to see. Corsey turned around, and reached behind him for the lamp.

"Let it burn awhile. I want to see you tonight." She said.

He left the lamp alone.

Reed rode hard away from the

meeting that day, before the sun fell below the horizon. After seeing Fisk in person he decided that putting as much space as possible between himself and Fisk for as long as possible was a very good idea.

Josiah didn't have much time to think as he was riding, but after stopping for the night he took time while building his fire to reflect on his overall plan.

Yes, John was dangerous, but Josiah's plans should eliminate any more need for direct contact with John. *My plans should also eliminate John's contact with anyone this side of hell*, he thought as his fire caught and he blew gently on the base of the shuddering flame. Not long after, he had a decent-sized blaze going. He settled down to wait.

Four men stepped into the circle of light thrown by the fire, and Josiah looked at each in turn. They approached with caution, but not with fear.

One was the leader, and he spoke first. "Took you long enough to get out here, Boss."

Josiah snapped a twig and tossed it at the fire before replying. His voice dropped most of the southern dandy drawl he had affected while hiring his other professionals. "If I wanted to know that you were resting comfortably, I wouldn't have arranged to meet you here, fool. If your beauty sleep is so important to you, there must be a great deal for you to catch up on and thus you all are in no mood to hear the details of the work."

Surprisingly, the other man didn't reach for the gun at his hip nor swing down the rifle he had rested on his shoulder, instead he hunkered down and made an attentive face.

"Always willing to work, Boss. What are we doing?"

Josiah leaned back, catching his knees with his hands and sighed.

"Killing them all." he said.

# NINE

Jones couldn't believe what he was hearing.

"Think about what you're offering for a minute, Marshal. Either I tell you how to get your hands on John Corsey and I go to jail, or I don't tell you and I go to jail busted up some. Either way I end up hung in some shit-poke town in the middle of nowhere." Roberts said. Jones face didn't show his surprise, but he felt it just the same. He shook his head.

"This isn't a negotiation Roberts. I'm saying you tell me, or I'll beat up on you before you get hung. Why die sore?"

Roberts crossed his arms over his chest and shook his own head. "I know you probably think I'm scared of pain, but remember for a moment that I'm a trained dentist. A man lives through pain, but not the rope. I'm willing to die sore if it means I didn't give up John Corsey to you. You're going to have to decide if you're willing to beat me anyway. I'll grant you that men can be made to break with enough pain, but do you really have the time, Marshal? How far are you behind already? Months? It could take weeks to break me, and where would you do it? Here, where I have visitors on a fairly regular basis and my men due back to the bunkhouse?"

Before Roberts could go on, Jones stood up and aimed the gun straight down Roberts' nose. Roberts' voice dried right up.

After a moment, Jones spoke. "What are you suggesting? That I let you go? One of the men who helped kill Jerry Brooks, just living out his days on a sunny horse farm? I think I'll decline your generous offer, Sunshine."

Roberts put his hands back on the arms of his chair, and Jones took a second to line up his swing before committing. It was still too fast for Roberts to get his fingers out of the way, and the butt of the gun smashed the first two fingers on his right hand to a bloody pulp. Roberts howled in pain and tried to stand up, but Jones shoved him roughly back into his seat. The Marshal had begun lining up a shot on Roberts' toes when the thin man managed to get his voice making words again.

"Wait a minute, Marshal! You've given me something to think about here—" The pistol's roar drowned out any other words Roberts might have had, and afterward he went back to yelling in pain.

The shot took the middle two toes on his left foot, and the blood was flowing freely. Jones had the gun right back in Roberts' face before he could react with any more talk.

"Now you listen here, Sunshine. There's no saying how far behind your friend and Miss Driscoll I may or may not be. What you should be concerned with is how willing I am to kill you one piece at a time until you tell me where to find them. I've changed my mind about the rope, coincidentally. Instead I'll leave you here, too busted up to move on in any hurry. 'Why?' you might ask, if you weren't too busy gritting your teeth against the pain."

Roberts was actually opening his mouth to interrupt, so Jones whipped him across the face with the barrel of the pistol, drawing a red line from right to left with the sight on the end of the gun.

"No talking back. The reason why is so that I can check out anything you give me on Corsey, and if it turns out false, I can come back and visit with you some more. Doesn't that sound like a good idea to you, Sunshine?"

Roberts wisely nodded instead of replying vocally.

"I thought so too. Now, am I going to have to shoot you some more, or do you have something to tell me?" Jones kept the gun on the other man. Roberts' lip had taken a bit of the side swiping blow from the pistol and he spat out a mouthful of blood before he spoke.

"He'll kill me if he knows I gave him up, Marshal. Not out of spite but because he'll have to, that's how his mind works. If I told you, I could tell anyone and he can't allow that." Roberts had more to say but Jones' patience to hear it had run out.

He punched from the shoulder with his left, a hard straight jab, and he felt Roberts' nose go when he connected. Jones shook his left a bit while Roberts bent double in pain. Though he couldn't see it, Jones heard the crackle of bones as Roberts reset his nose.

The Marshal meant business, and Roberts knew it as he shoved his nose back into place, and pinched the bridge hard, holding it with his right hand before sitting up, head thrown back as far as he could get it. He held up his left hand to forestall any further abuse. He cleared his throat once, twice, then leaned to the side to spit out a wad of mucus and blood. When he spoke, his voice sounded wet and nasal.

"Don't miss. He'll kill you." Then Roberts told his one lie, and Jones believed him.

Marshal Harvey Jones reined in

to call it a night, the day's events finishing out in his mind before he went to gather firewood. Sunshine Roberts was behind him, broken and bleeding. But still alive, for now. Jones was confident he could find him again if the man did manage to run away, the more pressing concern was Corsey, Lydia and Shorty's Hotel in Nederland, Colorado. As he set his kindling, Jones didn't even notice the bloodstains on his left glove.

# TEN

It took Corsey and Lydia two weeks to get to Louisiana from the *hacienda*. In the meantime, they picked up the four thousand from the dead drop. Corsey went to scratch an itch about Reed while Lydia was gathering the information for the night they would steal the painting.

Now, she walked from the turn out all the way to the white mansion. The big house itself was kept up immaculately as were the grounds directly around it, but in stark contrast the former sugar cane fields were a riot of wild plant growth; buzzing with insects and smelling of dark, wet earth.

The twin ruts of the trail were bordered on either side with these swamps in miniature, and they seemed stretch out to the tree line on both sides. It was hard to see from where she was, but she could tell that the fields ran all the way around the house. Lydia set her feet on the long trail leading up to the front hitching posts and tried to keep her mind in the place a serving woman would have it. As she neared the house, a wooden sign became visible on the right. Constancia, it read.

The house was intimidatingly big, faced with more glass windows than she had ever seen on any single building. The front was majestically decorated by huge columns and a second floor veranda. The veranda itself ran the length of the house and its rail, instead of simple wooden beams, was intricately carved with a fine design.

She stopped for just a moment, gathering her thoughts one last time before knocking on the door of the impressive home.

The story she and John decided on was mostly drawn from the truth of her past, at his urging. The more truth in the lie, he said, the more believable it was. Her name was to be Lydia Finnegan, and she was an orphan from a family that had gone to seek its fortune in the west.

Tragic circumstances and feeling that the life in the west was too rough for her temperament, caused her to come back east. Unable to find work in any of the areas near her family's old home, she had gone abroad as first a teacher, and then a common serving woman, which brought her to Constancia, seeking employ. John made her repeat it three times and then grilled her with questions about the story before giving his approval. Her thoughts focused on the night they had last seen each other.

"That's good. Any high in station southern woman shouldn't care, but the other serving girls will want to know, and they will ask you questions." He paused, deliberating something before continuing. "If there is a man of the house, certain things may be expected of the serving women. Your being white should keep that out of the question, but be prepared."

"What should I prepare for?" She asked when he didn't continue.

He looked at her for a moment. "For how you want to handle it."

Lydia, having killed two men for trying to rape her before running away with Corsey, began to get her neck up. "Suggesting that I lie with some strange southern man so we can get the floor plan of the manor house? Or that I kill him, like I did Daniel Washburn?"

Corsey kept looking at her, the same as he had been. "Suggesting that you don't act like you're acting right now, should it come up. Make up some excuse, add it to your story. Tell him you're on your moon's blood. Tell him you were raped nearly to death out west and can't bear the touch of a man, or that the savage red tribes taught you to drink the blood of any man who lay with you." He paused. "Just don't react like you are right now, or Lydia Finnegan goes right out the window, and Lydia Driscoll will have a heap of trouble on her head. Understand?"

She took a moment to absorb everything he said, thinking it through backwards and forwards before replying. "I understand. That's all my part, though. What are you going to be doing while I do all the heavy lifting on this job?"

He looked away from her, out into the dark. "Digging. Either digging up whoever Reed is, or if he means to cross us? Digging a grave."

She put away her memories, turned her mind once more to the task at hand, and strode purposefully towards the front door of Constancia. She was met by an elderly servant, a tall man with white hair, ebony skin, and a wonderfully tailored suit before she could knock.

"May I help you ma'am?" His accent was thick, but John had helped her to quell the instant and irrational irritation that such an accent would normally bring out in her.

She nodded brusquely. "Yes. My name is Lydia Finnegan, and I've come to inquire as to employment as a serving woman here in beautiful Constancia." She knew it wasn't really done to simply walk up to the front door and state one's intentions to a mere servant, but she wanted to get next to the servants as much as the other residents of the house.

If the tall man was taken aback he did a good job of not showing it, and he bowed as he opened the front door wide and allowed her in.

Lydia hoped the rest of her part of the job went as smoothly as getting through the front door.

Corsey guided his flat-bottomed raft into slower water as he approached yet another ramshackle hut on stilts set back amongst the waving and bobbing reeds. Talking to the people who lived in these places had proven just as difficult as he had imagined. They were deeply mistrustful of outsiders to their way of life and even more so of anyone not from the South. Corsey's gold had gotten him what little information he had. His gold was not in unlimited supply, however and he disliked using what Reed had given him on the job Reed wanted him to do. What he did know still didn't amount to much, but he reviewed it carefully before calling out to the hut.

The trail in Texas lead to a madam that would not talk to a man that wasn't law. Corsey was a lot of things, but he wasn't law. After three days' digging and not finding anyone who wanted to tell him anything the job was calling, so Corsey rode on.

Among the river rats and swamp dwellers community and family meant everything. Any folks coming through from Alabama would have been marked and noticed without failure by the entire river community, not just the plantation owners and their ilk.

He learned that Constancia had freed its slaves when the Emancipation Proclamation had come down from Lincoln. In fact, most of the information he had gleaned so far was from boastful white men who claimed to have 'hung me one o' them runaways my ownself'. Corsey didn't care one way or the other about slaves or the manor house, that was Lydia's part of the job.

His hand fell to his gun as he contemplated how best to convince this particular swamp dweller to answer his questions. Force worked with some, gold with others, still others were just glad to see another human face. He shrugged and poled his way over into shouting distance, leaving the gun where it was for the time being.

"Hello the house! Anybody in the house?" He waited a moment and saw a man walk out onto the shabby porch.

"What you want, stranger?" The man on the porch was wearing a pair of homemade trousers, held up with a rope over one shoulder.

"Just got some questions for ya, if ya don't mind." Corsey replied.

The man on the porch waved him over. "Come on up, I heard about you. Askin' questions all over, *oui*? Been expectin' ya."

# ELEVEN

Josiah rode into Louisiana about the same time that Lydia did, but he came from the west, instead of the north. The four men he had met with had long since gone their own ways, their orders clear. Being in Louisiana Josiah ran the risk of being recognized, and word getting around to Corsey. He had to count on the fact that Southerners were more likely to trust other Southerners, even rotten apples like Josiah, over any damn Yankee.

As soon as he crossed the state line Josiah started looking for a place to lie low until his plan could go into action, and he found that place soon enough. The whorehouse and gambling parlor had been a stop on his trip west, but he exercised a bit more caution in his dealings with the whores, being this close to home.

Bayou Charlie's was a two story building, one of the last standing in the decimated town of C'est la Vie. The war of northern aggression had hit the place hard, taking every man between fifteen and fifty into its brutal embrace. The women folk had mostly moved on, but some of the businesses had stayed profitable, with the men passing through, both blue and gray coats. Now that the war was over, few and fewer folks came this way, regardless of coat color. The last real business draw was Bayou Charlie's and people came in from the fields or the swamps for a night of carousing, and the proximity to a river inlet meant a steamer every now and again.

Josiah tied his horse off at the hitching rail and stepped up onto the boardwalk, kicking the clinging mud of the street off his boots and shaking the trail off his shoulders. When he deemed himself presentable enough, he walked through the open double doors of the place.

To his right lay the bar, with a bored bartender washing glasses. On the left were the faro, whist, and poker tables; craps had never caught on at

Charlie's. Straight ahead of him was a grand staircase that went up to a landing and then split off two ways up to the second floor, which formed a kind of balcony over the edges of the main room down on the first floor.

It being early in the day, about nine of the clock, the place was pretty well deserted. Just one old drunk at the bar and some tired-looking whores lounging near the staircase. Josiah doffed his hat to the bartender and approached the bar.

"I'd like a room for an extended stay, a bath and a woman to wash my back." He wasn't using his overinflated Reed voice, but his normal speaking voice, and the bartender warmed immediately, a smile on his face.

"Certainly, sir! Though a room will take some readying for your use, we can arrange a bath as soon as the water's been warmed. In the meantime, can I offer you a drink?" The man's face suddenly darkened. "I'm Charlie, owner and operator. I'm afraid I'll have to see the color of your money before I can approve your stay, Mister..."

Josiah withdrew a small pouch from his inner jacket pocket, being sure to open his coat far enough for the bar man to see his flashy gun. He pulled open the drawstring on the bag and reached in. When he brought out a single gold nugget the size of his thumb, Charlie's eyes went a bit wide and his smile came rushing back.

"Sir will do just fine, Charlie. I'll take you up on the drink, whiskey will do me just fine." Josiah spun the nugget slowly on the bar.

Charlie poured and then went to see about the bath, his smile never wavering. Josiah contemplated the four thousand in gold he had in his little pouch, and the four thousand he had left at the dead drop back in Missouri for Corsey.

The bank he used on his way through Kansas tried to scalp him on the exchange rate for his paper dollars to gold, and succeeded to a fair degree. He exchanged a letter of credit for ten thousand dollars for gold amounting to no more than nine thousand five hundred, and only that after a great deal of hemming and hawing, and a wire from the bank of issue in Alabama.

For once, he was grateful for his family name instead of cursing it. After he had the gold, he still had to find the drop-off for four thousand worth of the nuggets and dust.

John had given him directions, leading first from a town called Hays, then due east to a fresh water spring, then down the creek on the west side until he found a farm, burnt and ransacked during the war. After he placed the gold he was to fire a single shot, then ride on and after an hour of riding, fire another single shot. All this told Josiah that John was very cautious, very deliberate, and very, very good.

Josiah did what they had agreed to in the mud hut, feeling a bit foolish leaving four thousand dollars' worth of gold sitting in a blackened fireplace, under the hearth. The entire time he felt watched and measured, but when he came back later the next day, the gold was gone, and John had scratched 'Reed' into the hearthstone.

*A savvy operator indeed*, Josiah thought. They never discussed this part of it, but John must have taken it as a given that his new paymaster would want to know his money had been delivered and to the right man.

Charlie was on his way back down the steps, with a string of not quite dead young ladies in his wake, snapping Josiah out of his memories and woolgathering. He eyed the girls, and downed his glass of bourbon. He selected the woman who looked the least worn down and let her lead him to his bath.

# TWELVE

The last thing Lydia expected when she was led into the sun room of Constancia was the welcoming smile of her prospective employer, but that was exactly what greeted her. The woman sitting in the plush chair in the sunlight was swaddled in a blanket, despite the heat of the day. She was also the oldest white woman Lydia had ever laid eyes on.

"Sit, dear. Please. Tea?" the old woman said.

Lydia nodded solemnly, and with her hands clasped neatly in front of her, moved to the chair opposite the elderly woman.

"Thank you. I will have some tea, if you please. Shall I pour, ma'am?" Lydia used her best manners. The older woman seemed delighted with Lydia's courtly aspect.

"You are a vision, my dear, and so mannerly!" The woman rocked forward and back slightly. "Surely such a wonderful young lady has a name?"

Lydia decided she should pour, since there were no other servants in sight, and the lady hadn't stirred from her blanket.

"Of course, ma'am. My name is Lydia Finnegan. Do you take sugar?" Lydia's hand was poised over the silver sugar spoon. The older lady smiled again, creasing well-worn lines in her face.

"Well, this is a former sugar plantation, so I suppose it would be out of hand to decline the stuff entirely. So, just a dash Lydia, dear. As you probably know by now, having infiltrated my innermost sanctum here at Constancia, I am Geraldine Wilhelmina Beaumont." She shifted the blanket so it puddled in her lap. Lydia nodded politely, and scooped a bit of sugar into each delicate tea cup. The matriarch took up her cup, the saucer held shakily below it. Lydia did the same, taking the time to admire the beautiful pattern on the cup. Her awe wasn't feigned, as she reminded herself to not gape openly.

"This is a beautiful tea set, ma'am! Where ever in the world can this have come from?" she asked.

Geraldine sipped at her tea gingerly, approving of the temperature and flavor. "It is funny you should say 'where in the world' my dear. This particular tea set comes from Beijing, China. My great grandfather Aloysius bought it on one of his many globe trotting adventures." Geraldine watched as Lydia sampled the tea appreciatively before she continued. "I have to tell you that this tea has been my salvation from the rheumatiz that plagues me; it warms the very bones." They sat for a moment, enjoying the tea.

Lydia swallowed delicately, and took some time forming a reply, settling the cup and dish together with a minimum of noise. "It is wonderful stuff, ma'a—"

Geraldine cut her off with a loud side mouth cluck, more for talking to horses than to people. "Pardon the interruption Lydia, dear, but I simply dread hearing you call me ma'am any longer. Geraldine if you could manage, or Miss Beaumont if you can't, but no more ma'am! I simply will not tolerate it from those in my employ!" Geraldine said. Lydia smiled inwardly, for a moment. "Well, thank you, ma'a... Miss Beaumont. I must, in danger of sounding rude, inquire as to just why you have decided on hiring me, knowing no more than my name?"

"Everyone else assumes I must be infatuated with sugar. This, after all, being a sugar plantation, and me, after all, being a sugar king's sister. My point being that no one else knows how to make my tea, and I haven't the heart to tell them!" Geraldine sipped her tea slowly.

Lydia covered her mouth to hide her smile, but old Miss Beaumont broke out in guffaws of laughter. A serving woman, a dark-skinned woman nearly as old as Geraldine herself, came out of a side door with a scowl fixed firmly on her face.

"Now you jus settle yo'self down, you'll give yo'self a rupture like that, my yes you will!" The serving woman's accent was much thicker and more liquid syrup than Geraldine's dry tone. As much as John had tried to prepare her, she still had trouble listening past all the drawl.

"Delilah here minds me and helps me get from place to place, don't you Delilah?" Geraldine asked.

The serving woman replied. "I do. Not that you need any he'p getting' in trouble!"

Lydia liked these two old biddies, even if she was intent on getting her hands on what could be the most prized possession of the entire Beaumont clan.

She was placed among the white servants, in rooms in the west wing of the sprawling manse. Her duties were familiar enough, cleaning, serving and keeping her manners. She resolved that each night when she retired, she would write and drew a new room of the house into her journal.

# THIRTEEN

Corsey walked through the hole in the wall that served the shack as a door. His host began the conversation.

"Set yo'sef down dere, stranger. You got any whiskey in dem fancy saddlebags over yo shoulder?" The man who had been expecting a visitor smacked his lips loudly and rubbed his hands together eagerly.

Corsey sat in a rickety old chair and laid his saddlebags on an equally rickety looking table. Why or how the man had been expecting him was still unclear. Corsey had moved more or less at random, seeking any hint of Reed he could find. From what he had seen, the swamp folk were largely unwilling to talk to him, but crowed to each other like magpies.

Corsey took a bottle, wrapped in soft hemp rope to keep it from breaking, out of his bags. He uncorked it then set it gently on the table, keeping his hand on it. The swamp man's accent seemed to come and go depending on how much he concentrated so Corsey wanted him to concentrate. He kept his hand on the bottle.

"Name's Corsey. I'm looking to find out about a man named Reed. You know him?" he said.

The swamp rat tore his eyes reluctantly away from the bottle in Corsey's hand. He shook his head.

"Nawp. Not so's like you been lookin' for, anyway. Any other names you wanna try me with, Corsey?" the small dirty man shifted his seat, clearly enjoying being in control of the flow of information.

Corsey's eyes narrowed, this one had something to tell him.

"Reed, Josiah Reed. How's that one sound?" he said.

The man nodded his head quickly. "Sounds like a drink to me, Corsey. How's about you now?" the swamp rat was already reaching for the bottle.

Corsey nodded in turn and slid the bottle across to the man. "Sounds

about right. You got a name, fella?"
Corsey waited while the man took a
swig from the bottle, his eyes bulging a
bit.

He set the bottle back on the
table a little shakily, and wiped his
mouth with the back of one hand. "Call
me what you like, Corsey. I like your
whiskey, so I'll tell you what I know. If
you leave me the bottle." the man said,
keeping one had on the whiskey.

Corsey sat back. "Talk." he said.

The man grinned, showing teeth
that were a shade of green only slightly
less rancid than the swamp water
Corsey had paddled through to get to
the nasty hut on stilts. He watched as
the new owner of the whiskey enjoyed
another pull off the bottle before he
started talking.

"First off, the man you lookin' fo'
ain't the man you lookin' fo'. He
someone else altogether, Corsey." the
swamp rat was still enjoying telling his
tale.

Corsey waited to hear something
he didn't know. The only name he had
on Reed was 'Josiah Reed', which he

knew might be a fake. John also knew he didn't have another name. He used the one he did have, to find this man who was telling him things he already knew. Corsey made himself wait quietly.

"His name, it is Josiah, but not Reed, oh no, not Reed at all. He be well known to those hereabouts in the swamp. Musta come through lookin' for agents who wouldn't mind tearing away a piece of that Constancia by the river."

That drew Corsey's attention. That Josiah, not Reed, had looked for men to do the job he had hired Corsey to do in such a wretched place as this swamp, surprised him.

"Yes, Corsey, that got your neck up, *oui*?" The man chuckled through his rotten grin. "Maybe you don't think such as we here in de swamp be good enough to do the job you do, huh? Maybe you should think that job was a different job then from what it is now, just like Josiah Reed was a different Josiah then. Or maybe you don't think that, I leave it up to you."

The man reached for the bottle again, but Corsey shook his head once, sharply. "No. The name."

The man's hand started to shake as he drew it back to his side of the old table. His eyes showed whites briefly before he began dry washing his hands. "Maybe I think one bottle of your whiskey ain't payment enough after all. A dead man can't drink any whiskey, Corsey."

From under the table came a distinctive click. Corsey began to speak, "You're right about that fella. Seein' as how I don't know your name, I figure to put on your marker," Corsey's voice broke into an eerie simulation of the swamp dweller's. "'Greenteeth, him what was fond of whiskey, kilt by his mouf'." Corsey's voice returned to normal after a slight pause. "The name, fella."

The man shook a bit more, seemingly uncontrollably. After a moment he quieted and his shoulders slumped.

Corsey recognized that the man had gone sullen, a dangerous place for a man to be. Greenteeth might think that no matter what he was going to die, so why tell anyone anything? Corsey had to shake him out of it before he got too far down that path of thinking.

He quickly half-stood in his chair, and while leaving his right hand under the table filled with his gun, Corsey reached for the bottle with his left. He gripped it around the neck, grabbing it in a swiping motion, then brought it back across the man's face, hard. Some of the whiskey slopped out onto the table, and the air was suddenly heavy with the smoky scent of the liquor and the coppery smell of the man's bleeding face.

Greenteeth's attention seemed to be back on the here and now, for the time being. "Josiah Beaumont is his name, and he came here and tried to hire me to do his dirty work for less than you paid for that whiskey, Corsey." The bleeding man's voice was a bit thick with all the blood combined with his accent, but Corsey managed to make out what he said.

## Saint Lucy

It still didn't mean much to him, but at least he had a name.

# FOURTEEN

All Jones could think about as he watched a man die at the end of a rope was how much of a waste of time the whole thing was.

Two days after riding away from Sunshine Roberts' place he came across a little silver town where the silver had near run out. In such places nerves are worn awfully thin as peoples' stakes began to run low and silver claims began to dry up. Everyone in those type of places seems to just be waiting for the end, and that was a hard way to live, in Jones' opinion.

He was propping up the one bar in the one saloon in the dying town, laying the dust with a beer when a commotion started out front of the joint. For a moment, Jones considered leaving it be. He looked at the bar and the fading bloodstains on his glove. The Marshal pushed away from the rail and walked outside.

One of the locals seemed to

agree with the Marshal's personal philosophy about hard living, and had stolen a horse to ride out of town and start fresh somewhere else. Jones felt better about involving himself once he saw that his horse had mysteriously disappeared from the hitching post.

Of course the townsfolk would hear of nothing less than the man be brought before a justice and served sentence for such a terrible crime, and never mind that the closest courthouse was near fifty miles back in the direction Jones had just ridden. And of course there wasn't so much as a deputy of the peace to be had in such a going-to-hell little no-more-silver town, so who should draw the duty of seeing the horse thief before a judge but Harvey Jones.

Traveling anywhere with a prisoner is never easy, and traveling with a prisoner who knows he's most likely going to be hanged is the hardest kind to handle. Jones had to take to hog-tying the man to keep him from trying to hobble away in the dead of night, shackles and all. It got to the point that Jones was seriously considering offering the man his freedom or just shooting him out of hand, but the Marshal's sense of law and order got the better of him, this time. So he brought the thief before a judge, who was properly outraged that such a villainous type would try to steal a law man's horse, and gave the thief the rope for his trouble.

The horse thief twitched his last on the gallows, and Jones fetched a deep sigh. He wondered how far ahead of him this whole sorry episode had gotten Corsey and Lydia. He knew the trail was cold. Cold as ice after all this time, but it was distractions and situations like the one he had just dealt with that would waylay him unto eternity if he didn't find a way over and through. Having taken off his hat to see the horse thief off to his short drop and sudden stop, he now placed it back on his head and turned to where his horse was tied at the hitching post a few yards away.

# FIFTEEN

Josiah had spent a full week ridding himself of trail dust and wetting his end in the various sad-looking women at Bayou Charlie's before he got back to his plan. The four men he had met up with would have left a message for him by now, one way or the other and so he gathered up his bits and pieces of traveling gear and got ready to make an excursion. With his bag in hand he walked down the double staircase of the brothel and nodded at Charlie, who was behind the bar as usual.

"Be gone a few days Charlie, I would be glad if you didn't let out my room in my absence." Charlie nodded quickly, willing to do whatever it took to have the continued patronage of a spender in his joint.

"Yessir, we'll have it clean and ready for your return!" Josiah strode out of the front doors and to the small stable kept off to the right of the big false storefront of the place. He hadn't checked on his horse since bedding down the first night at Charlie's, and he hoped his two dollars a day had purchased his horse good care over the last week. The stable boy looked to be a halfwit, not uncommon when families mixed with their own as readily as they did in backwaters like C'est la Vie. His horse seemed well cared for, however, and Josiah flipped the drooler stable boy two bits. The animal had been saddled as per his request and he mounted up with the same unconscious flourish he used when dismounting. Turning the beast with a tug on the bridle and the tap of a heel, he set out for New Orleans. If the weather stayed with him, it would only take a few days to get to the city.

The port city was as bustling as he remembered it. Men and women in the latest Paris fashions walked the cobbled streets, studiously ignoring the tar stained sailors that stared at them. Even the servants that trailed along behind the elite looked down on the dock workers and sailors. In New Orleans, there was always someone lower than you to spit on. Josiah felt right at home.

It didn't take him long to reach his destination, a newly established wire office, once he was in New Orleans. A message was there for him, from the man in charge of the band he had hired. As Josiah read the message, a slow smile spread across his face. So far, so good he thought. The man he had hired, John, was making good time following 'Reed's' back trail, which was good, since Josiah had been careful to steer clear of using the Reed name anywhere near Constancia.

John would get little and less from questioning those in the area all while wasting precious time that he did not know was running out. The message noted that the group he had hired had lost sight of the man they were following a few times, but in the swamp such things happened. As long as John was hearing the right things, that being no things, all was well. Josiah was concerned that Fisk wasn't trying to puzzle out the house and the whereabouts of the painting inside, but a man as savvy as that would no doubt have some other way figured to get the information he needed.

Perhaps bribing a servant or kidnapping one, or perhaps posing as a visiting dignitary of some stripe. The only thing that really mattered to Josiah was that his 'hired man' not get a sniff of the real plan until it was too late. Josiah requested pen and a form to frame a reply to his group and began to write quickly but elegantly in longhand.

*Message begins: Continue tracking STOP Will signal when ready for big game hunt STOP Perhaps a measure of sugar needed for your resupply? STOP Report any strange movement of game immediately STOP Boss STOP Message ends.*

He handed it to the wire man and waited for his bill. The ride back to Bayou Charlie's was going to be a long one, but a trip into New Orleans like this was dangerous enough without trying to bed down in a place where he was so well known, especially among the whores and gamblers he would no doubt end up among. Even so, he briefly considered a taste of creole before leaving town. He dismissed the idea as quickly as it came. Late in the game was no time to throw caution to the wind.

The place was as rundown and the whores as depressed as he recalled, but Josiah took solace in knowing that his existence would not always be confined to cut rate prostitutes and rigged gaming tables, not with his plan progressing so splendidly. Still, at Charlie's he was safe from recognition. Despite knowing these things and his best efforts, that night his caution deserted him. Texas was too many miles away and to long in past. He needed a release.

The woman was the one he had bedded most often of the lot at Charlie's, and the familiarity had bred contempt in him. She had come along as readily as always, glad to make the money. She was undressing him, and already naked herself when his temper flared.

"Take your clumsy hands off me." His voice was quiet but rang like funeral bells in the stillness of the joint and the room. The swamp bugs outside the walls buzzed noisily, eerily.

She stopped undressing him, standing stupidly with her hands at her sides, head downcast. After a few seconds she began trying to cover up, angering him again.

He slapped her hands away, his hand making meaty-sounding impacts on her arms. He knew that hitting her at all was a bad idea because once he got started he could never stop, but he started all the same.

"I never said to cover up, idiot. Sit on the bed before you make me sick."

She sat immediately; cooling his temper somewhat, allowing him to take back a bit of control. He sat in the chair collecting himself for a moment, stepping back from the edge.

## Saint Lucy

He stood quickly, knocking his chair backwards. The woman uttered a breathy sort gasping scream. After that, Josiah could only remember the color red and a savage sort of joy.

# SIXTEEN

Lydia's journal was growing thicker as she added extra maps and floor plans, detailed with notes in her small, neat script. She used the English alphabet but wrote in a short hand, phonetic version of the language her fourth father had taught her on the plains before she had sought her fortune in the white man's world. Playing the serving woman came easily to her. She felt her fourth father would have disapproved and she hoped her prayers were enough to still any anger his spirit might feel over her subservience.

It was a week since Lydia had been taken on as a maid in the household, and she was waiting for some kind of communication from Corsey before making some pretext to disappear. She put the stylus aside and reviewed the information she had gathered as well as the final parts of the plan she had yet to carry out.

Lydia's work was mainly in the kitchen. The head cook was a rotund black woman that everyone called Momma Flowers. Lydia liked her very much. Momma Flowers was a tough, but fun master of her kitchen. She always left out a dish of cream for the cats and saved back the mixing bowl from sweet baked goods for the younger members of the household to 'clean out.' The morning Lydia had begun her mental map of the kitchen, Momma Flowers had noticed.

"You lookin' at them corners like they goan clean themselves, Lydia-girl. Here now, go on and get the dusters and we'll have it done." Momma Flowers seemed to take idleness as a personal affront. It was another thing Lydia liked about her.

Lydia's other main duty consisted of serving Lady Beaumont's tea and keeping her company. Geraldine's personal servant, Delilah often joined them. Geraldine liked to sit on the second floor veranda in the afternoons and talk about the old days of the plantation.

"All of this wild was once sugar cane, as far as you cared to look. You can still see the old slave houses there, buried in the creepers. See, Lydia? Not there dear, to your right." Geraldine gently corrected Lydia's gaze.

Truthfully, Lydia had been judging the height of the veranda and checking the sight lines from the windows.

"Ah, yes. I see them now. Thank you. Where did all the workers go once you freed them, Miss Bee?" Lydia felt a shock of fear as she accidentally used her pet nickname for the grand old lady out loud.

"Miss Bee! I quite love it, Miss Finnegan!" Geraldine laughed, "My husband, God rest his soul, would have told you I had quite the sting." The old lady recovered herself and answered Lydia's question. "They left here. Delilah kept in touch with some. The others... Well, you tell her Delilah. I can't bear to think of it in words."

Delilah, who was normally finicky about Geraldine's feelings, looked as if she didn't want to get into the details either. Her face was drawn and her voice was flat, sounding nothing like her normal, warm tone.

"Most got lynched, Miss Lydia. My own boy took his family off to live on his own farm and some fools in bedsheets hung him and his wife and they children off an old oak tree." Delilah stopped talking and Geraldine reached for her hand. They sat in silence for a moment and Lydia felt a momentary pang of guilt about why she was there, on the veranda of a grand old mansion with two wonderful old women who had lived their whole lives there. She waited for it to pass. It didn't, so she thought of her own past, the four different families she had gone through before landing in Crow Wing, California. She had met John there and made her choice, soaked in blood. After that, she knew she could do what she had to.

The other parts of the house were harder to access without suspicion. For the first week or so, she could feign getting lost on her way somewhere else. The third time she was caught by the doorman, who doubled as the carriage driver. Lydia learned his name was Simon.

"Miss Finnegan. Lost again? I see you have the afternoon tea service. You must be on your way back to the kitchens?" the man was icily polite. Lydia could handle icily polite. Suspicious was another matter. She had to keep Simon in the dark, so she showed him exactly what she thought he expected.

"Y-yes, sir. I've never served in a place so large before. I feel like I'm getting lost all the time." She put some stammer into her voice to show that he was intimidating her, even though she wasn't intimidated.

Simon shooed her away in the direction of the kitchen.

The white servants blended together in her mind. They were mostly the laundry and farm hands, jobs that at Constancia had traditionally been whites only. It seemed to please

Geraldine to have a white running with all her black house servants. She spoke of it over tea with Lydia, once.

"I knew it would be a different world after President Lincoln made his proclamation." Geraldine said, staring out over the rail of the veranda.

Lydia sipped her tea quietly, thinking how far away the simple problems of surviving were to the people who lived in these great houses on the river delta. She remembered finding the whole camp of her fourth father's people, dead of the smallpox. No proclamation would change their lot in life.

"Sadly, not much has changed. You're my little effort at changing things. You sleep in the same wing as the whites, of course, but you serve with Simon and Delilah and my cooks. We all must do our parts in the name of progress." Geraldine coasted to a gentle stop in her reverie.

"Yes, Miss Bee. In the West, the race lines are drawn differently. There, white men and red men fight, and the whites need all the help they can get."

Lydia checked herself, hoping she didn't sound too angry, or satisfied.

Lady Beaumont gave her a sharp glance, and was content to sip tea quietly.

Lydia was surprised to find her mind lingering more over the people she was meeting and learning about than the information she was supposed to be gathering. To dismiss them, she thought of John. He was counting on her to do her part.

After she had the layouts and locations of the house and exits down pat and on paper, she was to record the movements of the other servants, as well as any other residents in the house. A slight furrow creased her forehead as she thought about the reason she was in the manor: the painting of Saint Lucy, which she had yet to lay eyes on. It wasn't that Miss Bee didn't trust her. Instead she supposed that the painting was in a room only used to host guests or the like, of which there had been none.

Observing and mapping out the

servants' movements had been easy enough, the pretending to get lost several times had shown her who was in the house and when quickly enough. The old mansion's floorboards were full of cantankerous creaks and groans and she had begun to recognize the tread of the different residents on the noisy floor.

The communication from John was to be when he was ready, rather than when he judged her to be ready for him, but she worried. Not about being found out as a fox in the hen house, but for Corsey having to deal with the insular and mistrustful swamp folk. Her fourth father's people had legends about the swamp people and their mistrust for anyone from outside. The Seminole tribe were famed for their ability to confound their foes with the superior knowledge they held about the flooded deltas they inhabited. She supposed that white folk in the same surroundings couldn't help but develop similar tendencies.

Her thoughts turned back again

to John. If anyone could take care of himself it was that man. She knew he would come back to her, one way or the other. Thinking of John got her back to thinking of what the two of them planned to do in Constancia: Stealing a priceless painting from a kind old woman which supposedly held the secrets of ancient Aztec gold held back by the conquistadors from the King in Spain after they slaughtered the ancient race that minted it. She followed John's lead. The map mattered not at all. The payment for stealing the painting was their concern. To get that payment, they had to successfully steal the painting.

And they needed that payment.

It all sounded surreal when she looked at her part. A maid only, a serving woman in the big house by the river. Beneath all the maps and notes in her journal, she wrote her thoughts down; hoping to share them with John later as she would have had they been together.

# SEVENTEEN

Corsey was spending his last few bits on a shabby hotel room in New Orleans while he thought out his next move. He spent a week after he and Lydia parted in the swampy delta lands to come up with the name. Lydia would have the whole house mapped and measured by now, but Corsey still didn't know enough about Josiah's intentions to feel comfortable taking the painting out and just handing it over. It wasn't the painting, or what was or wasn't on it, but what Beaumont had planned for afterward that slowed Corsey up.

Pulling Lydia out wouldn't be easy in any case. If Josiah had watchers on the house waiting for the painting to come out, or if they had made Lydia for an agent it would be more complicated. He had planned to get her out using a telegram about a dead aunt or some such. That seemed a little too open now. If there was another crew out there, she would be walking right into them. He settled on contacting her by letter, dropped off by special courier.

He stood up off the bed in the cramped little room and took the single step to the foot of the bed, where his saddlebags hung from the bedpost. After a few seconds rummaging, he came up with a carefully wrapped bundle: ink pot, stylus and paper. The room's other fixture, aside from the bed, was a table and chair. He settled himself gingerly in the chair. The overall shabbiness and slapped-together nature of the of the place extended to the furniture. He started writing. As he wrote, he decided what to and what not to risk putting in his note.

The rest of Corsey's visits up and down the big river didn't give him half as much information as he had gotten from Greenteeth on that lonely bayou. Everyone else he talked to seemed more ready to give him two barrels of lead than a warm welcome, let alone information on someone they considered to be one of there own. The fact that the clannish swamp folk stuck together against him didn't tell him much, in and of itself. The look they all seemed to get—sort of scared and flinching—when they were not talking told Corsey volumes.

One thing that stuck in Corsey's head after he left Greenteeth to his hard earned whiskey was what job exactly Beaumont had tried to hire the swamp rats for. While Josiah was pretending to be somebody he wasn't he had never pretended to be stupid, and wouldn't have sent two groups after the painting. Had he been recruiting for the job of going after the supposed gold? The other question was whether or not Josiah had managed to recruit his other group. The whole job was starting to stink and Corsey briefly considered pulling Lydia out no matter the risk and riding on.

He dismissed the thought almost immediately. They had nothing to fall back on besides petty robbery, which was a good way to get hanged.

When his letter was done, Corsey folded it carefully and sealed it with wax dripped from the room's single candle. He put the letter and his writing bundle in the saddlebags and slung them up over his shoulder. Taking all his belongings with him whenever he left seemed the only likely way to keep them from being stolen. He made his way to the outskirts of town, looking for a stable. He kept to the more populated avenues. They were all done in hard cobbles and mostly free from the glutinous mud that made up most of the streets. On either side of the cobbled streets houses with fancy ironwork railings on their balconies rose up, shoulder to shoulder with each other. The lower element wasn't much in evidence. It wasn't that he was unwilling to face the robbers and cutthroats that thrived in the alleys, but killing anyone tended to bring in the law one way or the other, even in a city as corrupt as New Orleans.

The belles and their beaus owned the fancier parts of the city.

They walked, arm in arm, servants trailing along behind. Most crossed the street to avoid men like Corsey. They wore the latest Parisian fashions. He wore a gun belt and an old, sweat-stained hat.

He located a stable with a drunken hostler and a stable boy eager to make a few extra coins. Corsey paid the rent on the horse and gave the boy something for himself, half now, half when the boy came back, letter delivered. The plantation seemed well known to the boy, which probably meant it was well known to most of the locals. That bothered Corsey and he couldn't figure why, outside of the danger inherent to knocking over a well known local.

He put the worry aside and settled down to wait for the boy's return.

The hostler had woken up at one point. Corsey ignored him and left once the boy returned. Seeing the fancy rich folk had given him an idea. The only thing fancy types enjoyed more than frippery, lace, and perfume was gossip. A trick Corsey had learned out West when looking for someone was to stop off at the printer's office. Newspapermen were far less careful with secrets than telegraph operators, and kept just as meticulous files.

After several false starts that led him to the doors of newspapers that published in French, which he did not read, Corsey stood on Gravier Street, in front of a building with the sign 'The Picayune' hanging off the front of it. He walked through the door and put on his best hangdog expression. He wasn't much of an actor.

"Can I help you, sir?" A man stopped in mid-stride on his way elsewhere directly in front of John.

"My brother was kilt here some years past. I wonder if you all would still have his obituary around?" Corsey put some bumpkin in his voice. He could do voices.

"Come with me. Murdered you said?" The clerk led him to a side door that opened on a musty room. Without waiting for Corsey to answer the man said, "Here are the unsold editions. You're free to look through them, if you like. We've laid them by until a library takes interest in them."

Corsey looked into the room and turned to ask the man a question, but he had already gone. The room was stacked with crates and the crates were packed with papers. Some had months and years stenciled on them. Most didn't. Corsey chose one at random and started sifting through the papers, looking for any mention of Constancia or anyone named Beaumont.

# EIGHTEEN

The Marshal's progress across the territories, municipalities, incorporated townships and full blown states to his destination of Nederland, Colorado was slow. After the horse thief, there was a murderer and after him there was rapist and after him another and another. Jones was delayed and delayed further until he finally took to riding as far from civilized places as he could, stopping in at trading posts to restock his provisions and staying far from towns. Jerry Brooks and Crow Wing, California were much on his mind.

His conscience dug at him for those first few days, goading him with thoughts of things like dereliction of duty and abandonment of his post. Just like after he had beat Sunshine half to death in his pretty little country house, his guilt got lost somewhere between the vastness of the big blue sky and his thoughts of what he would actually do when he caught up with Lydia Driscoll and this Albert Fisk-also known as John Corsey.

At a trading post in Wyoming Territory, Jones' luck in avoiding his duty in favor of his personal crusade, ran out. The place was a two room shack, designed not much better than a lean-to with the larger end open to the elements. A worn table set at slightly higher than waist level ran around most of the three sides that were open to the air. A small aperture allowed passage from inside the counter to the out. A side door let out onto a front yard, and out the back a fenced in area kept a horse, two milk cows and three hogs from wandering off over the big plains.

When Jones rode up, the rough wooden poles that held up the roof on the large end of the lean-to were festooned with goods, and the counter was much the same, furs, blankets, sacks of dry goods. The Marshal nudged his horse over to the nearby hitching post. He was ready to swing down from the saddle and stretch his legs when what Jones assumed to be the owner-operator came bustling out from inside the darkness of the inner shack.

He was talking, but not to Jones. "You best not come out here where this man can see you, lest you'd like a belt in the mouth!"

Jones thought of intervening in the domestic dispute, but let the moment pass. "I'll be needing a fifteen pound bag of feed, and a new bedroll. The moths about got mine et through."

The trader's head bobbed up and down eagerly, glad to have the custom. He went about gathering Jones' order. While the Marshal might not have extolled the virtues of not beating one's wife, he did keep his eyes on the horizon. He did his best not to give the shop keep a reason to belt anybody in the mouth.

The Wyoming countryside was bland at best under the overcast sky of the day, the far off mountains were hazy in the clammy air. Jones' gaze scanned back and forth, and it was only because he didn't want to provoke a woman's beating that he saw the horse and rider break the monotony of the eastern horizon. The rider was coming hard for the post, that much was clear from his path. Jones could see whoever was sitting that horse was coming with a purpose.

The Marshal reevaluated his assumption about who the woman in the shack was. Clearly not a whore, or the trader would have offered, and several times by now. Possibly the wife or daughter or some relation to the trader, but then who was this rider coming hell bent for leather towards the isolated place? Jones loosened his revolver in its holster and reached down for his carbine, laying it across his saddle as the features of horse and rider defined themselves.

The horse was a bay with a white diamond on his forehead, a gelding from the look. The rider wore an ankle length duster, a broad brimmed hat and a whole lot of the trail. He or she was streaked head to toe in mud, dust and clean streaks left by rain. As the distance closed, Jones could make out clear tracks running down the strangers cheeks, cut there by rain, or perhaps tears. The horse was yanked to a brutal stop just a few yards short of the post's weathered counter. The rider jumped down, a very male sounding grunt coming from under the hat as the stranger gained his feet. Jones sat impassive, waiting for the next thing to happen.

The stranger spoke as he was pulling a double barreled shotgun from inside the bedroll tied behind the saddle. His voice was thick, likely clogged from trail dust and under use.

"Trader Mike, you get yore worthless, kin-stealing ass out here where I can shoot you!"

Jones considered briefly that Trader Mike had likely had better offers and trained his carbine on the stranger, who hadn't so far seemed to notice him. "Ease down, friend. I'm Marshal Harvey Jones and whatever dispute you have with the man inside that post will be settled under color of law. Put down that gun and we'll settle this."

The stranger looked Jones up and down as if seeing him for the first time. The shotgun stayed in his hands, but also stayed pointed at the dark entrance of the post. "I ain't never heard of you, and you ain't wearing no star I can see. How'm I to know you ain't just a friend of this kidnapping son of a whore?!" The stranger was clearly working himself up to putting Trader Mike down. After weeks of letting thoughts of Brooks' death rule him, Jones' sense of responsibility refused to let it happen.

The Marshal shook his head, drawing the attention of the dirty stranger back. "Don't make a stupid mistake, friend. I am a United States Marshal, and you will not be shooting anyone today, understand?" To make sure he was perfectly clear, Jones thumbed back the hammer on the short rifle and pointed it unwaveringly at the man.

# NINETEEN

When he woke the next morning, Josiah and the bed he lay in were covered in blood. The whore lay on the floor and her scalp was torn badly, revealing the red-smeared, bleary skull beneath. Josiah looked on her for a long time, and he was relieved to see her form rise and fall with breath. Relocating his place of residence at this late point in his plans would have been difficult.

Charlie proved accommodating and the injured woman was seen no more after that day at the whorehouse. Three days after that, a rider came looking for him, and Josiah got the latest news he was likely to get. Josiah needed to know when the thief was ready to strike. All the pieces were in place for him to execute his plan at a moment's notice. A plan that would return him to his rightful place. A plan that required his own hands to be publicly clean of the necessary bloodshed.

"Seems he's got wind of a rat, what with sending a message to the big house like he done. He spent the rest of the day at the newspaper. Mighta been lookin' for likenesses or sommat." The messenger had spun his tale quickly in Josiah's little room upstairs. Beaumont took only a short time to formulate a reply for the other man to carry back to the hired hands.

"More likely he's got an agent in the house. The dark of the moon is in two days, the best time for him to make his move. Come back here in a day and half with the men. They deserve a bit of sport before we get down to business. As to the men in town, I want that thief at the house on the dark of the moon, one way or another. But alive, you understand me? He's no good to me as a corpse. Until we hang him, that is."

The other man sketched a salute, not deigning to speak again. Josiah watched the man walk out dispassionately, all emotion spent the evening previous. Beaumont sat in the afterglow of receiving the news that his plans were proceeding apace. He reflected on his entertainments, his memory allowing now rather more than a joyous red haze. He had needed the release.

After the woman screamed, Josiah stalked towards her on legs that felt as if they were made of wood. She cringed away from him, and his awkward, lunging steps. Her fear only served to inflame him more and when he had taken the two steps across the room to where she sat, his rage was uncontrollable. He loomed over her, and she cowered before him. Her arms already covered her head and neck, but his right hand flashed out wickedly, knocking aside her defenses. When she turned her face up to him, he brought his forehead down with vicious intent, smashing her right eye socket into a ruin. She howled piteously, her body slithering limply from the chair where she had been onto the floor. Josiah stood over her, slightly dazed from the heavy blow himself. He kicked out at her absentmindedly and felt a few of her ribs let go through his boot. She groaned, which drew his full attention back to her.

His vision had been starting to clear but now the red haze descended once again. He kicked again, this time aiming very carefully indeed. The sick wet crunch when the pointed toe of his fancy boot sank deep into her already damaged eye silenced her.

He sat staring at the selfsame boot as he wallowed in his memory. They would all get what they deserved, one day. One of the whores, her eyes as big as saucers, had been standing in the doorway to his room for an unknown amount of time. The sharp movement of his head as he noted her presence tore a startled gasp from her throat.

"What." His voice was flat, and his face was clear of any emotion that the whore could see. Not knowing him, she decided to take those as good signs.

"Charlie says to ask if you want your lunch brought up to your room?" Her voice was quavering, but not as much as it would have been, had she seen the ruin her friend had come to for herself, Josiah reckoned.

"Yes. Now get out of my sight."

She vanished, and Josiah wondered if she had learned that trick from the rats she so closely resembled. He consoled himself with thoughts of what was to come. Soon it would be only the fanciest of ladies and the surroundings. Soon he would have what was rightfully his. Soon there would be blood enough to slake even his desire.

Close by a group of men sat around a campfire, waiting for the messenger to return. Some wore the ragged, patched remains of uniforms. Some didn't, but they all wore the same cold expression. They were hired for a purpose not all men could have carried out. Killing the defenseless, and more. Butchering a family tree so that all that was left was the youngest branch. They were hired for this, and for their silence afterward. It mattered to their paymaster that they all looked forward to it as much as he did.

# TWENTY

Lydia was washing the lunch dishes when Momma Flowers hollered out her name.

"Lydia-girl! You come on over to the back door!" Momma Flowers was drying her hand on her apron tails, blocking the view out the kitchen door with her considerable bulk. Lydia dropped her wash rag into the tub of hot water and stood up from where she had been sitting, cross-legged on the floor. She took a moment to brush off any noticeable dirt and food particles. Momma Flowers kept a clean kitchen and it wouldn't earn Lydia anything but a scolding to appear before the big woman with any obvious defects in her appearance. Straightening her apron as she walked she wondered what chore needed doing outside.

Momma Flowers was standing inside the doorway and frowning ponderously down at a grimy, grinning boy who was holding a piece of folded paper carefully where the black woman couldn't easily grab it away from him. Lydia put her best puzzled face on, even though she knew this must be John contacting her. Not getting into everyone's business always put Momma Flowers in a tyrannical mood, so Lydia kept her face fixed in a quizzical position.

"This boy here say he got a note for you, Miss Lydia." The other woman fixed her hard gaze on Lydia for a moment before stepping back from the door to allow the younger woman room to approach the boy.

"Thank you, Momma Flowers. And what do you have for me, young master?" Lydia put a little flirt in her voice and raised an eyebrow for the boy. His grin quickly dropped into open mouthed gaping. He seemed to forget how to speak, then gulped hard. It was clear he hadn't expected to deliver the note to a pretty girl. It most definitely was from John. The boy gulped hard and his eyes cleared a bit.

"A man paid me to bring this here to you miss. He said I should only let you have it and none other. He even sealed with this fancy wax, so's you'd know if I was peekin'! See?" The boy stuck out the note so she could take it.

Lydia sank down to one knee, bringing her to a height with the boy. She took gentle hold of the boy's arm. He jumped like a spooked horse under her touch and she fought to keep the impish grin she felt rising off her face. Her hand started at the boy's elbow and moved in a near caress down his arm to take the note. Spending time with the gossipy, rowdy, affectionate serving staff had given her a taste for the game she hadn't had before. If Momma Flowers wasn't going to demand to see the note, Lydia had to play.

"I don't have a penny to give you in honor of your brave service, young master. Still." Her voice had started low and gotten to a whisper on her last word.

His eyes were as big as saucers as she leaned in and kissed him on the cheek while plucking the note from his hand.

She lingered in her position just long enough to whisper, "Thank you." She stood quickly away from him, tucking the note into a pocket she had sewn to the inside of her apron. He stood still for what must have seemed like forever to him, then he shivered a bit and the sun might have shone out the smile he laid on Lydia and Momma Flowers.

"Thank you Miss Lydia! I'll tell your fella the note got delivered!" If his knees were a little weak when he turned around to leave, Lydia pretended not to notice. She turned around to face Momma Flowers, a demure look on her face now. As Lydia had expected, the other woman was covering her mouth with her hand and giggling fit to split.

"You one naughty white child, Miss Lydia! Lord you are!" The one thing Momma Flowers liked better than gossip was a good bit of teasing.

"A note, Miss Finnegan?" Simon said from behind the women. "I thought you had no relations near to here?"

Lydia was saved from replying when Momma Flowers spoke up in her defense. "Mebbe it ain't no relation, Simon. Mebbe Lydia-girl here's got one of the N'awlins beaus sweet on her! What you think of that, huh?" The big woman stepped between Lydia and Simon, shaking a wooden spoon at him. "Now git on out of my kitchen."

"Miss Beaumont will hear of this." he sniffed before turning on his heel and marching out the door.

Later that night, after Lydia had stolen away to her room, she broke the waxy seal on the note and read it, a hungry look in her eye. It was written in John's strangely perfect script, the letters and words and sentences arranged in flowing, even rows.

*Lydia,*

*I have been checking into our mutual business acquaintance, and have found only a few things of import. I believe you know as well as I do that means a great deal, as much as if I had found out many things, but in a different way. The major sticking point was that he used a name that was not his own, Reed, just like we discussed he probably had. I plan to close our part of the bargain two days hence, at twelve of the clock. I think it best to leave the livestock out of it, I hope you will agree.*

As I know of no other path, I will take established routes to get to my destination. I look forward to the end of our business with this man, and to seeing you again. One last item: The Reed name was false, as I stated, but the real name is as distinctive as Reed seems common. Josiah's real surname is Beaumont.

If you know or can find out anything about this name or our friend it would be a great help to us.

*Humbly and Sincerely yours,*
*John*

Lydia read it twice more just to be sure. She didn't know what it meant, but she knew it couldn't be good for the grand old house, and the grand old dame who was its mistress.

To keep the cold shudder that threatened to run up and down her back at bay, she reviewed what John was really saying in the letter. He would still do the job, approaching on foot and up the main road, at midnight two days hence. Lydia automatically placed it as the dark of the moon. Her mind came back to that impossible name.

All she had ever heard from the servants was that Geraldine was the last scion of her family, how sad, how sad. Who was this Josiah Beaumont?

# TWENTY ONE

The Marshal watched the stranger's eyes rolling like a horse's, when mad with fear or pain. He couldn't keep both Jones and Trader Mike's post in his view at once, and it was plain he considered both to be equal threats. Jones had decided there was probably some kind of truth at the bottom of the dirty man's accusations but the Marshal didn't know if the stranger, or Trader Mike for that matter, would live long enough for that truth to get sorted out. It suddenly came to Jones how he could find out what was what. There was someone he was forgetting about. The stranger was opening his mouth to start yelling again when Jones' ice cold voice cut him off.

"Enough of that shit, friend. Tell me your name."

Those wild eyes rolled back to the Marshal. "I still don't believe you is law, and I ain't your goddamned friend!" The double barrel shotgun the man on the ground was holding twitched a bit in Jones' direction.

The Marshal framed his reply with scorn. "Whether you believe me or not shouldn't matter to you as much as the fact that I will blow your head off if you point that gun at me." Jones paused to let the other man see he was covered, and that Jones' aim did not waver. "Now, I will settle this peacefully if you will let me. Put that gun down, and I'll get to the bottom of this right quick."

Those rolling eyes made another few turns back and forth before the stranger decided Jones was serious, at least about blowing someone's head off. The shotgun's front sight lowered, and the dirty man set the gun carefully down at his feet.

Jones nodded saying, "You've made the right decision. What's your name?"

The other man's throat worked a few times, and then in a nearly civilized voice he said "Brian. Brian Ludley. My cousin's name, she who

Trader Mike stole, is Mary."

Jones sat impassive, letting the unwanted answer hang in the air. Brian Ludley had the sense to scuffle his feet a bit.

Jones nodded again and called out to the post "Trader Mike! Come on out here, unarmed and smartly!" No sounds of movement came from inside the rough building at first. Shortly there was a single heaving sob, followed by a quick cry of pain.

Ludley made as if to stoop over and scoop up his gun but Jones was faster.

"Leave that goddamn gun on the ground, Brian. Mike! If I have to come in there without hearing your side, I'll figure you for being in the wrong." Jones let him think that over for a moment before adding, "You wrong is you shot, Mike!" Before Jones could do any more yelling or anything else, he saw someone moving in the gloom cast by the overhanging roof.

"I'm coming out, Marshal! I've got my rifle held up over my head!" the trader called out.

Jones frowned a bit, but what he got was about what he expected. The scrawny trader moved slowly into the light, his eyes blinking rapidly as they adjusted to overcast light of day. He walked out from behind the counter without being told and slowly bent over to set the rifle he had been carrying on the ground at his feet.

Jones kept him covered, but Brian Ludley looked ready to jump the trader and kill him with bare hands. Jones sighed inwardly and gripped his carbine one handed. He drew the pistol from its holster. Brian's eyes had switched over to Jones at the Marshal's first movement and as soon as Ludley saw Jones was going to keep them both covered, he forced himself to relax visibly. Before the inevitable imprecations could start, Jones took control of the confrontation.

"All right. Now, the facts I got are that Trader Mike has a woman in there of indeterminate origin." Jones motioned to the post with his head and continued. "Another fact is that Brian here believes that woman to be his cousin, Mary. He also believes her to be here against her will."

What could be seen of Ludley's face through the grime had gone first red and then nearly purple as Jones spoke. The Marshal thumbed back the hammer on his revolver and pointed it straight at the dirty young man.

"Calm down, Ludley. I have very little patience and you have nearly worn it out. Speak up when spoken to, to do otherwise will be at your own peril, understood?"

Brian's face went from purple to white as the idea that a lawman would shoot him out of hand sank in. Wisely, he nodded. Mike still looked as he had when he left the cover of the post: terrified.

"What I haven't heard is what Mike's side of it is." Jones looked hard at Mike, whose eyes kept darting back and forth between the two men he thought might kill him. If he showed to be lying Jones planned on shooting him. Abusers of women were some of Jones' least favorite types. Some of the appeal of this idea must have shown on the Marshal's face, because Trader Mike's knees began to tremor slightly before he started talking.

"I found her out in the wilderness all by her lonesome." From the corner of his eye, Jones saw Ludley's shoulders bunching up. "She said she was run away from home, on account of being..." The trader's throat hitched a few times. Jones watched that and Ludley's hands, which were bunched up into fists.

Harvey thought he had it figured but just to be sure, called out one last time. "Mary! Come on out from the post and we'll have an end to this one way or t'other!"

Mike called over his shoulder, "It's okay. Come on out." Out the girl came, and she looked to Jones to be no more than twelve or thirteen years at most. Her hair was bedraggled, but a pretty shade of yellow nonetheless. From the way she walked, he could tell she had been sharing her path with fear for a good long while. Her hands washed themselves endlessly against each other and her steps were cautious. She seemed to be trying to watch all of the men at once, but it was the one she looked at least that Jones was the most interested in.

He turned his attention to Brian, but asked his questions of Mary. "Is this man, Brian Ludley, cousin to you Mary?"

Brian lost some of the tension in his shoulders, but his chin went up a bit with pride, and Jones thought he could detect a hint of entitlement coming off the soiled young man. The girl's voice was quavery and filled with doubt. She very much wanted to give Jones the right answer, but didn't know what that answer was.

"Yes, sir." she said. She went on in a smaller voice, "But I was never kidnapped, like he said." Under Jones' eye the rage on Ludley's face was only a passing storm, but the Marshal saw it. Without a judge, Jones needed to be sure. He sat back on his horse a bit, giving relaxed body language, as if a weight had been taken off of his shoulders.

"She stays here." he said.

Ludley nearly went for the gun, but rounded on Jones at the last second, screaming "SHE'S MINE!"

The single shot from Jones' revolver echoed across the open countryside with the authority of thunder.

# TWENTY TWO

Corsey walked back through the front door of the hotel where his room was rented. The clerk let him pass by without molestation, Corsey paid for a full week when he rented the room and today was only day three. Walking up the stairs, Corsey could feel eyes on him. He stopped without warning. The whore leading a man up to her room behind him ran into Corsey's back and cursed. He turned, not acknowledging her, and looked quickly over the whole room.

The lower floor of the hotel was devoted to fancy women displaying their wares, along with a few gaming tables scattered throughout. At one of these tables, he caught a man who supposed to be playing poker just as his gaze shifted back to his cards. Corsey turned back and headed up to his room. Either someone had gotten wind of what he and Lydia were up to and wanted to deal themselves in, or

Josiah had set someone to watch his movements.

Neither option was a good one, and both made him want to find out exactly what Beaumont was up to. What he found at the Picayune offices only honed his suspicions. There were no articles about Constancia, and exactly one account in which a Beaumont was mentioned. The article mentioned briefly a gunfight at a place called Adelard's Saloon. The gossip column implied that the altercation had been over a woman. Corsey's hunch was that finding that woman would clear up a lot about Josiah.

In his room, Corsey shifted the chair to face the door and sat down with his revolver in his lap. He didn't think the man downstairs was there to do anything, but some people didn't think at all and Corsey was ready for that, too. Adelard's would have to wait until tomorrow. He had to figure the best way to lull his watchmen.

He briefly considered letting go of his itch. Knowing who Beaumont was didn't factor into stealing the painting and getting paid. Except now, there was a man downstairs who was set there to keep an eye on Corsey. The risks had changed. Someone was already sticking their oar in the water, muddying things up. Now it was riskier not knowing who Beaumont was, what angle he was coming from, than it was to find out about it. Corsey made his decision. He would go to Adelard's and look for the woman. The first step was identifying how close an eye was being kept on him.

He opened the door to his room and looked over the lower floor. The man who had been watching him at the poker table was still sitting in the same spot. Corsey spotted him before the man looked up and then made sure not to look at him anymore.

As he walked past the man's table, he heard the poker player say, "Fold," and start to push his chair back from the table. "Deal me out a few hands fellas, I gotta go to the privy."

Corsey didn't slow down as he passed, but walked out the front door quickly. He heard the other man's boots on the floorboards behind him, not running to catch up, but still keeping pace. Corsey went left out of the door and made his way down the boardwalk, stepping over drunks and shouldering aside any oncoming pedestrians.

The poker player's footsteps got lost in the din of the late afternoon street traffic, but Corsey knew he was still there. From the corner of his eye, he saw a man tipping his hat at thin air across the thoroughfare. A quick glance over the shoulder showed the poker player was indeed angling towards the privy, and settling his hat back into place. Corsey kept on, seeing the hat tipper following from across the street. There was more than one, and they weren't amateurs. They must have been behind him for some time, only finding them out now spoke to their professionalism.

Suddenly, Corsey turned into an alley. The muck from the gap between walks splashed onto his pants, but he didn't slow. He moved past crates and other detritus, making it hard for the man across the street to see him. He stopped and stepped behind a leaning piece of rough-cut timber, and waited. The hat tipper didn't bustle past him. So they weren't keeping a hard eye on him. They would know his major movements, and anyone he talked to.

Corsey walked out from the other end of the alley and made his way back to his hotel. He never looked to see if the poker player was at the table. These men were professionals, and Corsey needed to keep them fat dumb and happy while he looked for a woman at Adelard's Saloon.

# TWENTY THREE

Lydia spent the day after she had gotten Corsey's note sniffing around gingerly for any clue to who Josiah was. She started with her direct supervisor, Momma Flowers.

"It's just so sad, Flo. Miss Bee is all alone in this big old house, aside from us. Doesn't she have any family?" Lydia asked during breakfast preparation. The head cook's shoulders tightened momentarily as she worked a ball of dough for the day's bread.

"Nawp, it's just her and us left now, Lydia-girl. Everyone else is gone, dead and gone. Now you know Missus Beaumont do like a drop of honey in her grits, so goan get the jar from the pantry, hear?" Momma Flowers wasn't talking. Next on Lydia's list was Delilah, who she approached when they were clearing the lunch dishes and Geraldine was out on her veranda, enjoying the afternoon sun.

"Isn't there someone, Delilah? A

great-nephew or second cousin somewhere? I'd dearly love to meet a man with Beaumont blood. Miss Bee is so wonderful, I'm sure a man from her family would be kind and sweet and generous, like she is." Lydia had tried pity with Momma Flo, and it had gone nowhere. Delilah cared more for Geraldine personally though, and would respond better to flattery. Instead, Lydia saw Delilah's face go ashen and her lips thin down to a dark, angry line.

"No, there ain't a soul left. Clear these dishes back down to the kitchen yo'self, now." She hissed under her breath, looking to the door and checking that it was closed. Lydia knew all the white servants had been hired after the war. Because of that, they wouldn't know as much as house staff. She only had one option left. She had to talk to Simon. It would be risky, and she would have to play her part perfectly to avoid his suspicion. She decided to approach him during his nightly round on the ground floor to check that all the candles had been snuffed. She waited in her doorway, wearing her nightgown and brushing her hair.

"Simon." She greeted him idly as he approached, headed to his own room. As she had expected, he slowed a bit.

"Miss Finnegan. A good night to you." he replied.

"Wait a while, Simon. I'd like to ask you something." Lydia kept stroking out her long, black hair, making it shine in the light cast from the lamp he carried.

Unwillingly, he stopped and turned to face her. "Yes, Miss Finnegan? What is it?"

"Why aren't there any Beaumont men here, Simon? At my last appointment, the house was crawling boys, men and everything in between. It was a lively house." She locked eyes with the butler and kept the brush going, languidly. She knew she had made a mistake when his eyes narrowed and his mouth pursed in distaste.

"I see. There are no Beaumont

men to speak of. Not anymore." Simon looked briefly over her shoulder and remarked, "You keep a journal, Miss Finnegan?"

Lydia silently cursed herself for leaving her carefully kept notes open on the bed. Simon wouldn't be able to see any detail in the half-light of a lamp and a few candles, but now he knew that such a book existed.

"I'd wager there's some filthy, scandalous reading in there." Simon turned his nose up and walked down the hall to his room. Lydia listened to the door open and close, then closed her own door.

She only had one day and until midnight left.

Her plan for the night hours was to find the painting they were supposed to steal. By the process of elimination, she had figured out the room the thing must be in. Simon was always up the latest and the other servants had already bedded down for the night.

Lydia waited for two more hours

to be sure they were all asleep. She occupied her time reviewing her previous notes and her story if she was caught prowling about. Claiming she was lost at this juncture was no longer plausible. She hoped that she was trusted enough not to be instantly assumed to be trying to steal; having her inside the house to let Corsey in was half the reason she had assumed this identity in the first place. Lydia racked her brain, trying to think of what John would do but she already knew what he would have told her, *"Don't get caught."*

It was good advice, and she planned on trying to follow it.

The hour was up and she slipped out of her private room without a sound. Fifteen minutes before heading into the darkened house, she had snuffed her lamp to let her eyes adjust. Most of the windows were open, allowing what little breeze there was to pass through the house; the little remaining light of the moon trickled in. It was more than enough light for

Lydia to move by and move she did, sticking close to walls and the sides of the risers on the stairs to avoid being betrayed by the creaky old boards in the floors.

Her room was on the ground floor, and on the opposite side of the big house from the second floor room she wanted to examine. The single pocket on the front of her shift held a small, rough stone and a single match. On the other side of the house, the room in which she hoped to find the painting of Saint Lucy would be turned away from the light of the moon. She found herself in front of the closed door leading into the room.

Next to striking the match, this part of the search held the greatest danger of discovery. She had never seen the door opened, not even to clean the room beyond. If the hinges were rusted or tight, they would screech when she opened it. She muttered a quick prayer in her fourth father's tongue before attempting to inch the door open,

"Tate Ouye Topa, nauŋḣiuŋpi śni."*She grasped the cut-crystal handle and turned it slowly, the clicks as the tumblers drew back sounding only slightly louder than the thudding of her heart to her ears.

The door's hinges proved to be well oiled and maintained, making not a sound as she eased the door slowly open. She opened the door until it stood at a ninety degree angle with its frame, John had taught her that opening the door only far enough to squeeze through often meant you would knock over an inconveniently placed table or chair. Opening it fully meant that a person could stand in the space the door required, whether it was open or closed.

She was going to have to take a chance and hope that her brief match light would not be seen. The air inside the room was stuffy; the windows, if there were any, were not open. Lydia reached into the pocket sewn onto the front of her nightgown and brought out the match and striking stone. She

---

*"Winds from the four corners, let them not hear"

stood waiting for a few extra seconds, waiting to see if her eyes could adjust to the inky darkness in the room. When she was sure they wouldn't, she closed her eyes and struck the match, holding it over her head.

She must to be quick, the matchstick wasn't all that long. Lydia inched her eyes open, scanning around the room as her eyes re-adjusted to the sudden light. She saw the picture frame quickly, but couldn't make out the image without drawing closer. She had to be sure or all the risks she was taking were for nothing. Stepping across the room, her eyes picked out other details revealed as the light traveled with her. Dust lay thick on the round table and three chairs around it that centered the room as well as on the lamps, candles and other accoutrements in the disused room. Lydia strained her eyes to see the details of the image in the picture frame and could see it clearly as she drew closer.

The background was a heavy black, but the colors of the painting jumped out at Lydia: the girl's red blouse, her crown of flowers, the white of her shift. On the gleaming silver platter the girl held forth, Lydia could just make out two small orbs: Saint Lucy's eyes. The thing was too big for her to carry off alone. She would need john to help carry it and a horse to move it quickly.

Lydia shook out the match and reversed her steps as precisely as she could remember in the dark. Soon enough she bumped up against the door she had left open and could see the faint light of the hallway outside. Breathing a sigh of relief, Lydia closed the door slowly and made her way back to her room with the image of a young girl, not unlike herself, offering up her eyes to the Lord on a silver platter burned into her mind.

# TWENTY FOUR

It was a week since the trading post, and Jones hadn't seen another person since. He rode hard after that, knowing he had done right by the girl by getting rid of her cousin didn't help knowing he had done wrong by her by leaving her with the trader, even if she had thanked him. The post had been close to the border between Wyoming and Colorado, and Jones turned his horse towards the mountains in the distance. Nederland was said to be a gold town, and it sat up in the mountains a bit.

The air here was clear, so clear Jones didn't trust his eyes telling him how close those mountains were, he knew it would be a good bit of a ride before he was even into the foothills. As he rode he there wasn't much to think on besides why he was still chasing the two remaining Crow Wing heisters.

Lydia Driscoll had stepped off

the stagecoach and into a mess. Jones had known then that she hadn't been to blame, not for any of it. Even though he had known that, he had also known that there was more, much more to her than what any man could see at first glance. Given the powder keg that any mining town becomes, he was a fool not too see that Lydia Driscoll couldn't help but throw off sparks. He had let her go on about her business, and at the end of her stay in Crow Wing, California, two men were dead by her hand.

After eliminating all other possibilities, he figured that the only place the gold could be was with Lydia, hidden in her bags. Jones followed her into Sacramento, and watched her hotel like a hawk. He rattled her cage a few times, telling her how horribly the big outlaw and the fat outlaw had died, but she had not rattled. More than anything, that convinced him that she was in on it. Maybe not from the beginning, but she had been in on the end, he was sure of that. After she disappeared, Jones started down the long trail that led him here: Nederland, Colorado; looking for a joint called Shorty's.

It took most of a day to ride up through the switchback trail that led into town, and it was twilight before he passed a bullet riddled sign welcoming him to Nederland.

Jones reined up in front of the first saloon in town. The chancy evening light made the sign out front unreadable, but the raucous din coming from inside the place seemed likely enough. Jones swung down off his horse, grimacing at the stiffness in his legs. He paused outside the double doors, remembering his badge. After a moment's deliberation, he turned his collar up and pulled it off the inside of his lapel. Taking the time to pin the circled star to his jacket, he stepped inside.

The layout of the place was familiar, and Jones couldn't see any obvious threats in the souses on the main floor. As soon as a few pairs of eyes found him, the chatter and shouting started to dry up. He walked across the room to the bar, seemingly oblivious to the sudden quiet.

The barkeep stood washing glasses, but stopped when he saw the Marshal walking towards him. Jones kept careful watch on the man's hands, he wouldn't be the first bartender to keep a sawed off under the bar in case of trouble. For his part, the Marshal kept his duster on, covering his pistol. When he reached the bar he leaned forward on it, his hands on the top.

"Barkeep. What's the name of your joint here?"

The man behind the bar settled visibly when he saw both of Jones' hands on the bar, holding the Marshal up.

"Annie's Nugget, Marshal. What, uh, is there anything you need?"

Jones looked around amiably. "Looking for a place called Shorty's here abouts. How do I get there from here?"

The bar man looked blankly back at him. "I never heard of it,

Marshal."

One of the older men started wheezing, and it took Jones a moment to recognize the sound as laughter.

"You know something I don't, old timer?" Jones turned around. His amiable look was gone.

The old timer's wheezing tapered off. "Plenty I know that you don't Marshal. About this Shorty's: seems I remember that place from coming west. It's clear across the territory, hunnerts of miles from here, in a town called Clear Water."

Somewhere, Sunshine Roberts was running.

# TWENTY FIVE

Josiah could deduce his hired man had someone inside the house from the news the tail had brought. He had planned on executing all the servants regardless, but now he made a mental note to find out which one John had managed to turn. Even one day of waiting had passed excruciatingly slowly for Josiah, since all the women were too afraid of him to spend the night in his room, or even share his bed. He had thought about forcing one or two, but none had really looked worth the effort. So he had waited out one day in his room, and the following day he had spent waiting for his men to arrive and readying for his 'emergency ride' into the city.

The killers he hired would be arriving any moment. The timing of the thing is the trickiest bit, Josiah thought. It had to be the dark of the moon. His gut instinct told him that was when his thief would move. He needed his hired thief to have already stolen the painting, or even more precipitous, for the man to actually be in the house. Even if Josiah wasn't that lucky, he had plans to get the thief on the scene the night everything was set for. All that remained to be seen was how big a mob could be drawn out to the old house to confirm Josiah's side of the story before they lynched the thieving murderer. Beaumont's anticipation was palpable. He would finally get what he deserved.

Josiah checked his appearance one final time in the mirror above the bar as his men walked into the saloon, and the only thing colder than the smile he allowed himself were his flat, black eyes.

# TWENTY SIX

Josiah's men were watching him, so Corsey couldn't approach anyone who might have information on the man without some sort of pretense. When night fell Corsey went to work, ignoring the unobtrusive tails following in his wake.

He was looking for Adelard's, which wasn't difficult. He avoided the classier joints straight away, and concentrated on the places closer to the docks. He felt more than saw the different men trailing him through the streets and tucked a thought away again about their professionalism. Pushing past the still heavy foot traffic on the dockward streets it didn't take long to find a place that would have drawn a man like Josiah Beaumont like shit drew flies.

The flaking sign out front read 'Adelard's Saloon' in the flickering torchlight that provided illumination in this part of town. The place had once had a grand old storefront. Now it leaned dangerously out over the muck of the street; pieces of wood hanging from it threatened to fall away with every gentle breeze off the nearby gulf. The double doors on the front of the place were chocked open with some dead man's boots and an out-of-tune piano competed with the hoots and hollers of the patrons for supremacy of ugliness.

Corsey walked through the open doors and looked for a woman men might've fought over and saw her sitting with her back to the piano, a bottle clutched in her hand. Her whore's costume was stained and ragged, and the puckered, purple scar running from the corner of her right eye back to the ruin of her missing ear explained the lack of attention from the obviously lusty crowd. Corsey walked directly to her and held a hand down in front of her face. As if to confirm his suspicions she flinched heavily, dropping the bottle to the floor. Tucked between his fingers were two heavy golden coins. When she was done flinching, she licked her lips at the sight of him and took the offered hand up.

The room was worse than the one he had paid for in his flophouse, but it was mostly the smell. The light cast by the not oft cleaned oil lamp on the bed stand was kind to her, and for the first time he could really see that she had been pretty once, even beautiful.

It was there in the way the light caught in her hair, and the line of her neck. Someone had done his work well however, and the scar jumped out soon enough. He could tell she was broken inside, and that would make her hard to question. It was unlikely he would be able to use fear or pain against her. When she had the lamp going to her satisfaction she began pulling her stained shift up over her head but stopped when he held up a hand. She stood for a moment, not knowing what to do until he began to speak.

"Sit down. I just want to talk to you. I'll still pay, but what I need is answers."

She did so, slowly, clearly not understanding.

He decided to take the quick approach. "Beaumont."

She moved jerkily but quick, as she pulled open the drawer in the bed stand and yanked out a knife.

Corsey sat down on the floor Indian-style and set his hands on his knees.

"Talk only. What's your name?"

She shook minutely.

To get her attention he laid the two gold coins on the floor in front of him. She visibly wavered on the edge of attacking him in her fear, but sank to her knees on the floor in front of him instead.

She jammed the knife into the floor and spoke, "C-Cassie. How... what do you want to know about him?"

"Did he do that?" he asked, motioning to her scar.

She wrung her hands in her lap. "Yes. He done other things, not just to me. He hates us, mister. From how he talked right before... Before he done this, he must hate the whole world and every person in it."

Corsey got the rest of the story out of her in fits and starts. Beaumont was dispossessed of his inheritance over being the bastard son of a cavalryman that called on his mother while his father was away at war. When the truth came out, Beaumont's father killed Beaumont's mother and then himself. Josiah blamed his mother, and by proxy, all women. After what he did to Cassie at Adelard's, the rumor was that he had been disowned by the family and told never to return.

He walked out of Adelard's with all the information he needed and a big dopey grin on his face. He hoped it looked real, but didn't really care. He normally didn't put on airs for men he knew he'd have to kill. With what he knew now, there was only one way out, and it led down a trail of blood. He had all the pieces to the puzzle that was Reed, and they formed a picture of survival. Either for himself and Lydia or for Beaumont and his demented dream but not both. Never both.

## Saint Lucy

He got back to his hotel, and sat in on the poker game long enough to start a fight with Beaumont's hired professional. When it was over, Corsey had one less man to kill.

# TWENTY SEVEN

Just like in Sacramento, it was the waiting that made for the hardest part. Lydia had been over and over what John had written in his note and it didn't make one day and until midnight pass any faster. Momma Flowers had walloped her with a wooden spoon before breakfast was even served for dragging her feet, but she couldn't shake the feeling of time dragging right along with her. Afternoon tea seemed as if it would never arrive. When it did, it failed to brighten her mood though Geraldine was as chatty and engaging as usual.

"You seem quiet today, Lydia?" Geraldine settled her cup and saucer on the small table between them on the veranda and raised a quizzical eyebrow.

Lydia gave a small smile and motioned at the tea pot inquiringly. "I, yes. Miss Bee, I'm just worried about you. This big house seems so empty."

Geraldine waved away the offer for more tea and smiled back. "How could I be lonely here with our Momma Flowers, Delilah, Simon and you, dear? You all fill the hours and keep quite delightful company. You must think Simon is a terrible fussbudget, but he's quite the mind for chess. Delilah and I have quite the little book club and then there's afternoon tea with you."

Lydia had been making conversation, filling time until the interminable waiting was over with. She found herself feeling a pang of regret that she would have to leave these people, the first people she had let herself get close to since meeting John. Afternoon tea hadn't helped as much as she hoped.

Lydia moved through the rest of her second to last day in *Constancia* as if in a fog, until Delilah grasped her elbow while she was sweeping in the kitchen and whispered in her ear.

"You come along now, chile."

Lydia went along willingly enough, propping the broom in a

corner as she passed. She barely had time to wonder what the other serving woman could have to say that couldn't be said in the kitchens when she started to recognize the route they were taking through the house. The last time she had walked it had been in the dark, but it still lead directly to the disused room with the painting of Saint Lucy hanging in it. Lydia spoke up, "Where are we going Delilah? Is something wrong?"

Delilah squeezed Lydia's elbow a bit tighter but made no audible reply. The other servant reached out for the knob and turned it slowly. With a dry snap and a gentle push, Delilah opened the door to the study and the contents were as Lydia remembered them: table, chairs, and dust undisturbed from her last visit.

Delilah put a small but strong hand on Lydia's lower back, ushering her into the room. Lydia walked in, her mind ablaze with questions, and her face a careful study in calm curiosity as she studied the room in daylight. The windows were closed but not locked, although entrance or exit from them would require a ladder, as the room sat on the second floor of the manor house.

The study was noticeably lacking in feminine touches, clearly a man's leisure room. Of course, Saint Lucy still hung on the wall, her offering to the divinity of one young man's soul staring blankly up from the silver plate in her hand, and a demure look on her face. Lydia was turning, round and round and finally spoke in a whisper, "What are we doing in here, Delilah? I've never been in this room. The dust alone could attest to that..." Lydia, in keeping with her character of Lydia Finnegan, crinkled up her nose and made to start cleaning the room.

Delilah shut the door softly behind herself, turned to face Lydia, and spoke in a low voice, "No cleaning now Miss Lydia, not in here. This was Missus Geraldine's son's private study, and she asked that nothing here be disturbed. I brung you in here over you askin' questions about *that boy*."

Lydia quirked up one of her

eyebrows, showing some real curiosity. She noticed that Delilah didn't use his name, but she hoped she was about to learn something about Josiah. She decided to shrug it off and play slightly coy.

"I just found some dusty old toy soldiers and thought Geraldine might have a strapping young grandson squirreled away somewhere, perhaps abroad at school, or some such." Lydia stopped herself before she said anything else. Delilah was already frowning heavily, and John had taught her about lying right along with loving.

The trick was to say as little as possible, but still make the lie sound as if you really believed it. Keeping your lies simple meant they were easier to remember and using the truth made every lie told more believable.

Delilah had let the moment of silence stretch out, and Lydia reminded herself to fidget. Her time with her third father and her fourth father's people had taught Lydia patience beyond reckoning when dealing with what she thought of as

'Waśiçu'* and fidgeting was as alien as the railroad, to them. Lydia smoothed her apron front over and over again looking only rarely at Delilah, waiting for the other woman to speak.

Finally, the syrupy drawl Lydia had been waiting for broke the heavy quiet, "We don't talk about *that boy* no more. Not ever. He done wrong, so wrong I can't even tell you Miss Lydia. If you ever meet a man who says he is *that boy*, you run." Delilah paused for a deep breath

She went on, "Run as hard as you can in the other direction and pray he doesn't catch you, because *that boy* was pure poison. The man he became is worse, if that's even possible. So don't you talk about him, or ask about him or even think about him no more. You understand me now girl?"

Lydia had let her eyes focus in on Delilah as she spoke. With each descriptor of Josiah, she let those eyes get a little bigger and a little bigger, until finally they felt like saucers. When the older woman finished, Lydia

---

*People other than us, also refers to white language.

blinked slowly and nodded meekly. She opened her mouth to say, "Yes'm," but Delilah had already turned away and was shooing Lydia out of the open door.

A few seconds, a whirl of skirts and apron later; and Lydia stood alone in the hall with the dire warnings from Delilah ringing in her ears. Where tension had been singing in her stomach, now dread hollowed her out. One half of a day and until midnight.

# TWENTY EIGHT

Josiah's men, save those watching his other professional, were there at Charlie's sitting around one of the poker tables on the otherwise empty gambling floor. Josiah made sure not to remember any of their names, instead assigning them designations based on a memorable feature. Pox-scar sat to his right, picking at his fingers with the tip of a battered, but still very deadly knife. To Pox-scar's right there was Rider, still in his bedraggled Confederate cavalry uniform, to Rider's right sat Bowler Hat, to his right Hawknose sat tall and proud as his red man heritage would let him in the company of white men. Completing the circle, on Josiah's left sat Patchwork, whose jacket was made from the blue scraps taken from the uniforms of the Union soldiers' throats he had cut. Josiah made sure not to remember any of their names, and so pointed a finger at Pox-scar.

"Your part will be coming in the servants' kitchen entrance. Be sure to be quick, quiet and over all, careful. I don't want my house burned down." Beaumont gave a thin chuckle that passed around the table a thinner smile and continued, now pointing at Bowler Hat.

"I hear you're best with a rifle, so you'll be out front of the house. Anyone trying to escape should be an easy target for you, but pay special attention to the pathway leading up to the house. Any passerby that comes down that trail to investigate will have to be dealt with before they can preempt my panicked ride into New Orleans." Bowler Hat nodded solemnly and sat back to listen as Josiah pointed to Hawknose.

"You'll have the harder part of it, I'm afraid. After he," and Josiah hooked a thumb towards Pox-scar, "gains the entrance in the kitchens, you'll have to stalk quietly up to the second floor and deal with my Grand-dame and any servants currently up there. Nothing sets the Negros to running like knowing the mistress has had her throat cut. Remember too that our soon-to-be-hung thief should be about somewhere." Hawknose sat unblinking and unmoving for several long seconds while Josiah waited for some kind of acknowledgment or sign of understanding. Finally the native tipped his head down slowly and just as slowly brought it back up to level, the slowest nod Beaumont had ever seen, but a nod nonetheless. He continued by pointing out Rider,

"The rear of the house will be yours. I suspect the grounds keeping has been sub standard since my sweet grandmother freed all my rightful property at the behest of a fool in a stovepipe hat. So, pay special attention to avoiding disturbing the overgrown shrubbery and get yourself noted before the game is truly afoot. I don't suspect too many will try the back door. The river has been slowly turning my beautiful gardens into just more swamp back there for some years." Josiah lowered his pointing hand and turned to face Patchwork, he was the de facto leader of these lawless men, and so he merited special attention. Josiah made sure not to remember his name.

"For you, the most important job of all. Be sure our thief is safely bundled up and ready to face the justice of the howling mob I plan to assemble. Your men, who even now remain in town watching our mutual friend, should be warned that he is not to be taken lightly. All precautions need to be taken that he not slip the net. He knows too much to be running loose while we do his dirty work." Beaumont turned back to the rest of the group and concluded,

"That should sum up all your portions, gentlemen. Are there any questions before we adjourn?"

Patchwork's voice sounded as sewn-together and horrible as his grisly jacket looked when he spoke up, "Just leave us to this other man's work, boss, and we'll not disappoint. Now, we'll show you what you need to know about our bona fides."

The men got up from the table

and spread out, drawing knives and pistols as they went. Josiah could not afford to have been seen with the men who would 'find' the inhabitants of Constancia being slaughtered. When the screams were over, the till overturned and the whiskey spilt, Josiah set the first flames himself with a shattered lamp. The memory of the night sky lit by the jumping flames that ate Bayou Charlie's, Charlie himself, and all those in his employ had kept Josiah in good spirits for the entire ride to the city on the river delta.

# TWENTY NINE

The door to his hotel room burst in at a quarter past nine.

"What's all this white shit on the floor?" a man wearing a Confederate States cap whispered hoarsely.

"Ssst, idjit!" a man in a pork pie replied. From above, all Corsey could see to identify them by were their hats. One had on a distinctive Mexican sombrero, and the last two wore flat brimmed, new from the store jobs with fine leather bands. The men were professionals, they did not come through the door firing shots and they had the window exit covered from below.

The five men surrounded the bed quickly and began pummeling the man-shaped lump under the blankets with the stocks of their guns. The lump lost its shape and Bowler hat threw back the thin blanket. The sound of creaking wood in the rafters of the room caused all the men to look up in the stunned silence.

Corsey started with sombrero, who had stayed by the door. He had Lydia's Winchester repeater, and it belched fire and death into the room below him as he worked the lever action. Pork pie flopped forward, a bullet passing through the top of his head and tearing away most of his jaw.

Corsey chose the order by who stayed and who ran. The men who stayed died first. Confederate cap shouldered a scatter-gun, looking to wound rather than kill. Corsey shot him through the chest. One of the Flat Brim boys went for the window. He got one in the back that sent him careening through the glass and hanging over the shattered pane.

The hole in the ceiling plaster was twice as big as Corsey needed it to be, and he shifted around to get a better angle on the remaining Flat brim. He went for the door, turned, drew and fired a pistol through the ceiling. Flat brim was hoping to hit something and give himself some cover. Corsey shot him in the shoulder.

The man fell back against the wall, cursing. Corsey worked the lever action and fired again. The man's throat exploded in a gout of blood. Screams could be heard from the rest of the hotel now. It would have to end quickly, if he was going to get away.

There was one man left outside the door, the lookout they had posted in the street. Corsey listened to him through the thin walls of the cheap hotel.

The man's breathing was heavy. Corsey couldn't see what kind of hat he wore. "What in the hell—who are you? I don't give a good goddamn how the boss wants you. I'll come in there, and I'll kill you, bastard!"

Corsey drew his revolver and rested the rifle on his leg. He pulled both triggers simultaneously and dropped down out of the ceiling onto the bloody, mangled bed. He holstered the revolver and walked slowly to the door with the rifle at his shoulder. A tell-tale spray of red drops on the floor outside told him he had hit his mark.

The man was lung shot, a bad

way to die. Corsey fired the rifle a last time as he passed, putting the man out of his misery. He noted the man wore a Texan style cowpuncher lid.

Corsey thumped the butt of the rifle on the bar to get the barkeep's attention. The man half-stood from his hiding place behind the bar, smiling weakly.

Corsey reloaded the rifle. "My bags."

The bartender put the bags on the counter and pushed them forward. Corsey dropped a small pouch filled with some of the gold dust Josiah paid he and Lydia for the job. The shining grains spilled onto the bar.

"The man who did this, where can I find him?" Corsey asked.

"I—I don't know, sir."

"Good answer." Corsey hefted the saddlebags onto his shoulder and walked out of the hotel for the last time. He had until midnight to get to Constancia, and Lydia.

# THIRTY

Marshal Harvey Jones rode east towards Clear Water, Colorado and cursed Sunshine Roberts for a liar. He cursed John Corsey for everything that had happened back in Crow Wing. Most of all he cursed himself for a fool. He had known Roberts was too smart to make up a big story about what had happened, but Jones hadn't known Corsey, and hadn't listened to Sunshine's words about the man.

The dentist turned outlaw turned horseman had told Jones the pat truth when he said that he couldn't give up Corsey. Roberts had said it in so many words. Jones rode hard for Shorty's Hotel in Clear Water, and prayed to the wrathful God of the Old Testament that Corsey was there waiting for him.

It took him too long to get across the territory. Jones found nothing of Shorty's Hotel but blackened timbers and a smoking hole. The Marshal's inquiries about a man named Corsey had led him nowhere, but it seemed some of the folk in town could remember the raven-haired, hard faced beauty who had accompanied some anonymous man. Jones discovered the owner of Shorty's, a Shorty Jacobs, had survived the fire that claimed his hotel, and relocated somewhere back east. Jones knew he was back where he had started, with not a whole lot to show for it. United States Marshal Harvey Jones waited for a time in Clear Water for his quarry. While he waited Jones sent a wire out, looking for Lydia, or Corsey.

What came back was something Jones thought he had left far in the past. Before Crow Wing, before the cow towns out west. What came back sent a chill down the Marshal's spine and his mind spinning back to a hard time and a terrible place. A place called Camp Douglas.

Finding Lydia and Corsey would have to wait.

# THIRTY ONE

It was full night when Beaumont arrived in New Orleans and put on his best stricken face. He had long ago given up trying to understand the hows and whys of people's emotions, but he could still pantomime them at will. His suit was stained and dirty, his face contorted in fear and his steps were wandering and stuttery when he entered the low-end saloon. He could feel eyes on him as the barroom chatter slowed to a murmur, then died out entirely. He timed his next move so that all eyes were on him, for maximum effect.

Josiah fumbled aimlessly across the saloon and the with no warning, crashed to his knees and started to sob.

One of the nearby men grasped his shoulder and asked him,

"What's wrong son?"

Josiah looked unseeing at the man's face and very quietly said,

"Help…"

The man shook Beaumont none-too-gently and replied, "Help with what, man? What happened to you?"

Josiah let loose, a gut-wrenching, grief-filled, soul-rending scream. He had heard them torn from female throats often enough to imitate one near perfectly.

His voice hoarse he began to speak, "My family… out at old Constancia…" He shook his head violently and batted his hands outward, as if trying to wave away the horrible images in his head. "They, they've been butchered. Killed in their beds, and in the halls and butchered like hogs! The blood! It was everywhere!" His voice slowly gained volume until he was screaming at the end of his rant, and the entire saloon had their eyes glued to the scene.

The man who had taken his shoulder had pulled his hand away as if Josiah was on fire when Beaumont had started screaming, but now he took a grip once more; this time with a hand on each shoulder. "Who did these things, man? Tell us!"

Josiah had hidden his face in his hands and now he pulled away from that concealment just enough to show them all his eyes, and for a moment he let them see what he really was: a man turned inhuman by the things he had seen. The crowd would never know that he had done those things himself or that he had looked on them with great pleasure.

Josiah replied to the man, but really spoke to the room, "Only one was still there when I arrived, I could hear him moving about, stealing, firing his gun into the mutilated bodies of my poor sweet..." he feigned a retching sound in his throat, and bent double to hide his smile. After a moment he continued, "I ran in terror. I took my horse and rode from there to here in a blind panic, but now, in the company of you good people, I have found my courage. That man could still be there, and if he is I believe justice should be wrought upon him!"

Josiah stood, straight and tall as he could, shaking off the false fear and horror to replace it with false courage and a very real killer's confidence. He looked all around at the silent crowd. They were ready. "If you brave and honest folk, who have taken me in here in my worst moment, would have that justice done, I say ride out! Ride out with me to Constancia and catch this man up before he slips away! Catch him up and show him we men and women of the South still know how to punish the guilty!"

The crowd roared, the men immediately stood to and made for the door behind Josiah, whose grim face hid a cold satisfaction. He hoped things at the big house had gone smoothly. For his plan to work and the forged will of his grandmother to kick in, all the people at the house would need to be dead. For Josiah to walk away clean with what was rightfully his, John would have to swing.

# THIRTY TWO

Night had fallen when Lydia heard the first screams. She was dusting the dining room, and so the voice of Momma Flowers in the kitchen next door was easy to distinguish. People have many different sounds they make, and Lydia had heard quite a few of the horrible ones in her hard life so far. Fear and terror are easily recognizable.

Lydia judged the hour to be late, most likely past eleven, but surely not midnight. Besides that she knew John wouldn't get himself caught by Momma Flowers. The door to the kitchen burst open. The round form of the head cook stumbled out and even in candlelight, the blood was easy to see. Momma Flowers won't be screaming or joking or gossiping or teasing anymore, Lydia thought as she dropped the feather duster and ran for her room.

John had sent her into Constancia with her pistol and her

knife. She had protested, at first. Now Lydia thanked his foresight as she dug into the bottom of her travel case for the knife. Momma Flowers had been killed more or less quietly. Her scream could have been put down to burning a finger or seeing a rat in her kitchen, and so Lydia guessed the man who had done it had wanted to keep his killing stealthy. Her hand closed around the handle of the knife she had taken from a man called Tom after killing him in a place called Crow Wing, and the door she had shut behind her opened.

Lydia looked over her shoulder, being sure to put a healthy dose of fear into her face. The man stood in the door frame, his features obscured by shadows until he stepped back into the light, motioning Lydia out of the room.

He spoke,"Come on out girl. Never mind about that fat nigger, she was going to up and cause a ruckus, but you're plenty smarter than that. Come on out an' I won't hurt ya."

Lydia nodded her head quickly, looking at the man's pox-scarred face and the hand hidden behind his back. Her experienced eye spotted the blood dripping onto the floor, and the spattering of trail he had left behind him. She left reached for the small purse of coins John had given her against the need to bribe anyone in the house. She gave him eye contact to keep his attention where she wanted it. She jingled the small coin purse as she turned. He started to grin at the sound of the coin, the pox scars on his face stretching grotesquely, and she took a step towards him while letting her eyes get big.

She pleaded with him, "Please sir, this is all I have in the world, please don't hurt me. Take it, I beg you, take it and leave me living!"

His grin grew impossibly wide as she stepped into reach, and he put his hand out for the money.

Lydia held out a badly shaking hand as he drew near and dropped the purse on the floor.

The pox scarred man's ghastly grin disappeared as he immediately began to bend over, and Lydia took the chance she had planned for. The man's neck was exposed as he bent over. Lydia made sure she aimed her stroke square before driving the knife deep into the big artery pulsing below the man's jaw.

He made a small sound of surprise, and she grabbed his hair and made a swift stroke across his throat, cutting off any further sound. She stepped back as he dropped in front of her, his last breath burbling out of his cut throat. She waited until he was dead to drag him into her room.

Lydia tucked the pistol under her apron, and the knife was at the nape of her neck, hidden from view by the fall of her black hair and held there by a simple leather tie-down. She noted no other screams as she readied for whatever might come next, but she had no doubts that the man that killed Momma Flowers had not come alone.

Her earlier conversation with Delilah echoed in her mind, talking about how the poisoned son.

She shed her Finnegan disguise completely before she left her room, and smeared the blood of the pox scarred man beneath her right eye in a solid, steady line.

Lydia had made friends in Constancia, and one of them was already dead. Working in the big house for the amount of time she had had given her certain advantages, and she avoided all the creaky boards and noisy steps that might have given her away. Moving through the halls, Lydia saw the white servants, none moving or breathing or living, though some still leaked blood onto the floor. She hadn't heard a sound of any of this. The killer or killers must be very, very good.

Her plan had been to try and lull any attacker she chanced upon by displaying no weapons, much as she had killed the man outside her room, but the sight of the other dead servants, along with the lack of accompanying sound, made her abandon that ploy. Whoever was at this butcher's work was no one to be fooled with. Lydia took the pistol out from under her apron as she crept along the hall leading to Geraldine's rooms.

She could see the double doors that opened on the mistress' sun room standing ajar. She moved carefully to the right side door; keeping her form blocked from any view inside the room.

A sort of shuffling could be heard, and the patter of dripping liquid that Lydia guessed was not water. She held her pistol and checked the knife in its hiding place before silently pushing the door open.

A single shot and the tinkling sound of broken glass told her someone outside was shooting in. It was followed by two fast shots that echoed from out front of the house. Lydia forced herself to be calm, forced herself not to think about what time it was and what those shots might mean.

In the sun room, Lydia saw a man's back in the light cast from the hallway. His shoulders shifted beneath the smooth leather jerkin he wore. Lydia recognized the dress that Delilah had worn earlier that day, now badly stained with blood. Delilah's feet kicked feebly, occasionally scuffing as they made contact with the floor, and her blood ran freely from some wound the man holding her up had inflicted.

The man dropped Delilah to the floor with a meaty thump; her throat had been cut raggedly across the windpipe.

He turned and Lydia caught a glimpse of deeply tanned skin and a hawk-nosed native profile before she started pulling the trigger of her double action. The man's body jerked as three of her shots slammed into his body, but he kept turning, and coming for her. He held a knife in his hand, barely visible beneath the heavy layer of blood coating his entire arm.

Lydia saw him see her, saw him note the mark below her right eye as he started to reach for her; she spit on the floor at his feet and spoke. "Ṡni kat'a."*

Her next shot needed to be her last. The man had the reach, the strength and the knowledge of close-in fighting to take her down. She aimed

---

*Your killing is done.

196

carefully, with her arm extended. The hawk-nosed native man was moving slowly, but with deadly purpose, towards her. She started to ease the trigger back, squeezing it gently, and saw the flash of the man's knife a second too late.

# THIRTY THREE

The original plan was done. Corsey rode as planned, knowing that Beaumont would still be waiting for word from the dead men in the hotel. Corsey had to try to keep his approach quiet; his and Lydia's best option was sneaking away from the whole mess. He left his and Lydia's horse tethered just beyond sight from the road. He walked back out to the road, and moved down to the head of the path that led up to the old house. Light was limited. It was the night of the new moon.

Corsey stayed to the left side of the path, walking on the worn wheel rut to cut any sound. The heavy wild growth just beyond the tree line chorused with ambient noise, but he knew these men were good enough to not only to note any extra noise in the night, but also the sudden absence of the noise of crickets, frogs and the like. Not knowing the number of Josiah's crew, save that after New Orleans they were less by five, Corsey had come with his own weapons and Lydia's rifle slung over his shoulder.

The path up to the house was long and well manicured, but not oft used. The grass grew right up to the indents of the wheel ruts on the path, and the trees had grown together overhead, turning the dark into pitch black. Corsey moved carefully, picking his feet up only enough to creep slowly forward. The path was well kept, however, and he hit no branches or obstacles as he inched towards the few lit windows he could see at the far end.

One of the squares of light was suddenly obscured, and Corsey froze as a man on horse back was silhouetted in front of the lit window. The shadow lifted something to its shoulder and after a moment fired the rifle it had been aiming. Flashes of light reflected off the glass the bullet had broken. Corsey sank down to one knee and put the rifle to his shoulder. The shadow shooter was taking aim at another window now, picking targets as they passed in front of the light. Corsey took a deep breath and waited.

The shadow went still as it aimed and Corsey squeezed the trigger. The two men fired. It was nearly simultaneous, but only nearly. Corsey watched as the shadow rider tumbled to the ground with half his shadow head blown away along with the shadow bowler hat he wore. Corsey had to rely on the idea crew like Beaumont must have put together to do work like this would enjoy it; their blood would be up. That, and that somewhere on the other side of all that blood Lydia would be trying to get to him.

He rose to a half-crouch and started forward again, keeping the rifle held at port arms as he went. The house was no more than forty steps away when three shots rang out quickly from the second floor of the house. Corsey was on the wrong side to see the flashes from the gunfire, but he knew the sound of the gun to be Lydia's.

He started to run flat out when

another gun shot sounded, and he was pushed rudely face first into the nicely kept front lawn. Corsey fought to keep from letting frustration, anger and pain cloud his thinking. He let the rifle go as he rolled into a somersault with the fall. He felt a wet warmth running down from the wound and soaking his pants. He clenched his fists against the pain and sagged to an awkward sitting position. His vision swirled with red as the bullet wound caught up to him.

A grating voice called from the darkness over his shoulder, "I dunno how you done for my boys in town, but you best sit right 'chere till the boss man come with his posse to do for you. Lest you fancy dyin' by gettin' shot a piece at a time." The man who had shot Corsey kept a light tone, a tone that didn't suit his voice, but all pretense of lightheartedness fled with his next words. "Now toss me that iron on your hip."

Corsey's hand moved to the gun butt and he briefly considered another alternative but instead drew the pistol slowly out of its holster, holding it with two fingers, letting it hang from the grip. He tossed it underhand back behind him and waited for what came next.

"Good. Now stand up straight and let me have a look at ya."

Corsey gritted his teeth and got his good leg under him, he braced himself by folding his hands onto his knee to push himself up and stood without falling over again. With a little distance from the shooting, he could feel that the wound was torn on both sides. The bullet had gone all the way through; he could also tell the shot had taken him on the outside of his leg, near the knee but not into it. Corsey stood balanced on one leg and let the shooter decide what to do next. He put a some wobble into his stance to show some weakness. It had the desired effect as he could hear the scorn in the other man's voice.

"Bind that wound and we'll get you out of sight so the boss man can decide how best to show you."

Corsey nodded weakly and pulled his handkerchief from his back pocket with an exaggerated slowness. He made a bit of a show keeping his balance, taking a hop now and then and letting loose with a low moan of pain each time he hit the ground. He chose not try the patience of the man with the hard voice. Corsey would likely only get one chance at him. Corsey began tying a tourniquet above the wound in the low light from the house. His one chance was coming. He had to be ready for it.

# THIRTY FOUR

Lydia's shots threw off the native man's aim, and that was what saved her. She spun around from the impact of the blade sinking into her left shoulder, and fell heavily, losing the gun in the process. She heard the man walking through Delilah's blood as he approached her, but her spin had put her facing away from him. Lydia shifted her weight from leaning on her arm backwards onto her rear and took a grip on the hilt protruding from her shoulder.

It had sunk in near to the hilt; she sucked in a breath through her gritted teeth and drew it slowly out. She felt rough fingers twining into the hair at the back of her head. She gave an unfeigned gasp of pain and surprise as the man yanked her to her feet.

She tried to grab the hand pulling her hair but her arm fell back down before it got halfway up. Lydia heard a dry chuckle from the man who held her, and she felt him step close in, felt the heat of his body against her back. Her arm dangled uselessly at her side, and her good arm was raised, cocked back over her head to claw at the hand holding her.

She saw his gore-covered arm coming around her body with a fresh knife meant for her throat.

Lydia made her move. She ran her hand down the back of her neck. The knife had stayed where she had hidden it through getting knocked down and she freed it from the sheath. She was trapped by his arm coming around, and would have to settle for a stabbing motion. She just needed something to stab.

The man's knife was coming inexorably forward, aiming at a point just below her jawline; right beneath her ear.

Lydia could feel his breath, puffing hot against her neck and aimed her knife thrust at where she judged his face to be.

She felt the tip of the knife skip off his teeth, but her strike was strong.

The knife slid up his face, slicing easily. Her third and fourth father, as well as John, had taught her to keep her knives sharp, her weapons ready for battle. The knife scraped along the man's cheekbone as he recoiled. He shoved her violently away, his hand going to his face.

Lydia's fingers started to get cold, and a lightheadedness had come over her. The man's shove toppled her again. She fell to the floor and looked for the gun. She shook her head to clear the spots from her vision. She half dragged and half crawled to where it was.

Already the man's footsteps were quick behind her. She put on a burst of speed, slithering like a snake, and grabbed the pistol. She used her momentum to spin around and fall on her back, bringing the ruined face of the native back into view. She heard a shot ring out from in front of the house, and steadied her aim.

She squeezed the trigger once, and the man's head snapped backwards. As the world began to go

206

gray, Lydia heard the spatters of the back of his head hitting the floor and wall. His body fell all a sprawl, landing half on top of her. Had she the strength remaining, she would have pushed him off.

The barrel of an ancient muzzle loading gun poked out from the doorway that led into the sun room, and the end of it shook badly. A dry voice called out, crackling with authority, from behind the gun.

"I have a gun, so you'd best get on out of here!" After a few seconds without any reply, a very unladylike grunt came from the doorway. "Hunh. I'm coming out there now, and any burglar I see will be a dead burglar shortly thereafter!" Geraldine Beaumont walked on unsteady legs into the sun room turned abattoir; the gun slid from her nerveless fingers when she saw Delilah and Lydia. Tears began to run down her face but she made not a sound. She went to her old friend and confidant, kneeling to cradle her head tenderly.

Jesse VanDeWalker

Movement caught Geraldine's eye, and she shot to her feet with an audible wheeze of pain as her joints flared with agony. The big Indian on the floor was moving weakly, and Geraldine meant to put a stop to it. She picked up the muzzle loader and stutter-stepped over to where the man lay, cursing her age and infirmity inwardly. Geraldine pushed the sight end of the barrel into his back, and was about to pull the trigger when she saw Lydia's eyes snap open.

"My word, child! Look out, this brute has some life in him yet!" The dame's mouth set into a grim line as she settled the gun back into her shoulder, but stopped again when Lydia spoke.

"No he doesn't, Miss Bee... Others may come soon, though. Help me move him, we have to hide until... Until it's over."

"Are you hurt, dear?" Geraldine gently examined Lydia's shoulder. "You've been stabbed! Did this awful man put that blood on your face?"

Lydia felt the last of her ties to

208

Miss Finnegan dissolve when she answered, "No, Miss Bee. I did." She sat up, putting pressure on her shoulder. "We need to talk about what's happening, but first I have to ask for your help in bandaging this."

Geraldine's eyes narrowed, but she dropped her gun again and set to doing what Lydia asked her to.

# THIRTY FIVE

Tying the wound off would afford Corsey the best opportunity to strike. He carefully rolled his bandana into a tube and wrapped it around his leg. He pulled it tight and made ready to cinch the knot down hard. He took a deep, shaky breath for the benefit of the shooter who still had a gun pointed at him. Corsey yanked the ends of the fabric hard causing a flare of pain, and fell to his good knee. The shooter watched impassively, waiting for Corsey to stand up so they could be on their way.

When he stood up Corsey drew the knife in his right boot smoothly, and, with practiced ease, flicked it at the shooter. Corsey heard the action on the rifle pointed at him work. He threw himself forward in a roll, pushing off his one good leg to where he had thrown his pistol. The rifle cracked out a shot, missing Corsey but hitting the pistol he had been diving for. Without a gun, Corsey went right for the man. If his aim had been good, and the man's reaction slow, the shooter should have a knife sticking out of him somewhere.

The shooter worked the action on the rifle again, but threw it away when he saw Corsey coming for him. He reached toward his belt and came out with a heavy knife, suitable for cutting seasoned leather. Corsey smashed into the man at waist level in a dive, and they both tumbled to the ground in a heap, the man's knife arm went up and down once, the second time, Corsey's hand shot out to grip it by the wrist, and gave a lightning fast twist to send the blade flying away.

Corsey was diving for the man, he saw the shooter reach for his knife, and had seen how the man favored his left side. Corsey ran his hand over the left side of the man's body, an oddly intimate motion, until he found the knife, sticking out of the shooter's left leg. Once he had a good grip, he twisted the blade in the wound and yanked hard, drawing the blade across the huge artery in the thigh. Battered, stabbed and shot, Corsey stood up as the shooter, who wore a jacket made of patches, bled to death on the beautifully manicured lawn.

Corsey retied his leg bandage, picked up Lydia's rifle and his pistol. The gun looked to be usable. The shot that had sent it flying only hit the wood grip, leaving a deep score mark but no mechanical damage. He limped his way towards the house as quickly as he could, hoping to get under cover and to where Lydia was before any other of Josiah's gang found him. The front door was tightly locked so made his way clumsily to where he figured the kitchen and servant entrance to be. He had taken the knife high on his back, had felt the blade slide down his ribs and then home just below them. It was a wound he couldn't bandage himself, and it was bleeding heavily.

He entered the house through the kitchen and saw a fat negro woman dead on the floor, her body holding the door to the dining room open. He heard hoof beats go around the other side of the house. At least one of Josiah's gang was still outside, and about to find the two dead men out front. Corsey stood still for a moment and decided to take a chance.

He spoke the language he had learned for her, from her. His mastery of it was imperfect and he said, "Kuwa wanna uŋhdapi Lydia. Çaŋtewaniça akiçita naġi iyaye."*

Corsey heard hushed voices from the second floor and moved slowly to the steps. He swayed unsteadily and gripped the banister to keep from falling. When he looked to the top of the steps to see how far he would have to go, he saw her there at the top of the stairs. She was covered in blood, with her mark of honor streaked beneath her eye. Lydia rushed down the steps, and he had time to see her arm in a sling before he collapsed.

---

*Lydia come here we're going home now. These hardened killers are all dead.

# THIRTY SIX

Lydia moved as fast as she was able. John had a makeshift bandage cinched around his leg and he was bleeding heavy from some wound she couldn't immediately see. He crumpled while she was still coming down the steps to him, and her heart skipped a beat. In the time she had known him, nothing had been able to stop him or even seriously slow him down. She felt a sudden flash of guilt knowing that John would've been able to ride away from Josiah's scheme without a look back as soon something smelled off if not for her.

As she reached the bottom of the steps, she knelt and gently turned him over, seeing for the first time the stab wound in his back. Lydia quickly grew frustrated with having the use of only one arm, and then Geraldine was there, working with an urgency and manual dexterity that belied her age and condition. Lydia leaned back and the older woman began tearing strips from Lydia's serving woman's apron to staunch the blood flow from John's back. He twitched when Geraldine swabbed at the wound, and Lydia sighed in relief when she got a clear look at it. It didn't look to be mortal, or welling with the tell-tale black blood that signaled a punctured liver.

"Go on and fetch me back a sewing needle and thread, dear and we'll try to put Humpty Dumpty here back together again." The calm tone in the old woman's voice was something Lydia hadn't expected, but was grateful for. She rose carefully, still not quite as surefooted as she was used to being, and went to do as she was bid.

They had John stitched up and laid him comfortably in a bed just when the noise outside the manor house started. The voices of shouting men and screeching women carried a long way in the quiet country night. The two women in the mansion heard the crowd coming a long way off.

Geraldine rose unsteadily from where she was sitting next to Corsey and walked slowly to the bank of windows facing the manor's approach. In the dark of night all she could see were the bobbing torches and the occasional flash of gunfire as some overeager member of the mob discharged a weapon.

She turned to Lydia, her face grave. "Do you think he can stand, and more importantly, can he run?"

Lydia stood and took up her rifle, checking the chamber for a cartridge. "I've no doubt he can stand, Miss Bee. But he will not run. Neither will I." Lydia turned towards Corsey, and saw his eyes were already open. "John, they are coming."

He pushed himself up. "Yeah. It'll be Josiah along with a crowd he's pulled together to hang us for killing the folk here." His face paled with effort and pain as he used the torn muscles in his back to get upright. "Alongside that, there may be some of his gang left yet. No doubt Josiah's told them out there that we've killed you missus," he said, indicating Geraldine. "The safest place for you is going to be in front of that mob, where he can't kill you and blame us."

Geraldine's mouth set in a grim line and she stood a little straighter. "I've not had the pleasure of making your acquaintance, John was it? Lydia's told me you came here to steal my Saint Lucy. There was some further hogwash about a map to Aztec treasure. You should know that my grandson is a very dangerous man. I'll go before this crowd, but before I do I need to know that Lydia will be safe, and that before this is over, my grandson will be dead."

Corsey held the gaze of the old woman for a few moments before he spoke. "Lydia will be as safe as I can make her, but we're partners and she'll take her share of the risk. As to your grandson, I can promise he won't live to cross me again."

The old woman nodded slowly.

Lydia had already begun to drag furniture and flip tables in front of the lower windows, doing it as quietly as possible. Corsey watched the old woman's face as her comfy home was torn apart and saw nothing there but determination.

"Keep the mob busy as long as possible." he said.

# THIRTY SEVEN

The rabble was responding quite nicely, but when he saw the dead bodies of Bowler Hat and Patchwork he knew his plan might be in trouble. He had to know how things sat inside the house: If his grandmother was dead and chiefly whether or not his men had secured his would-be thief for hanging. Josiah stayed at the head of the mob, pointing out the dead men.

"Here and here too, no doubt men come to investigate the many shots being fired at the end of the trail and killed by the selfsame murderous bastard who I heard stalking the halls before I fled!" The crowd roared its anger and frustration, there were near thirty men and a gaggle of women trailing along behind, hoping for a glimpse of the killer kicking his last at the end of a rope. Up ahead Josiah could see a rope, tied up in a noose, swinging from the old oak out front.

At least that much had gone

according to the plan. The more he thought on the two dead men the more agitated he became. Josiah couldn't imagine anyone in the house putting up such resistance, aside from the possible agent John may have slipped in, and that left John alone to account for the bodies. Somehow, someway his hired guns had underestimated his hired thief and now Josiah needed to know the situation. As his rabble got closer, he heard hoof beats coming from around the back of the house, towards his position.

"Ready your weapons, good people! Someone's coming!" Few in the crowd had guns of any reliability, most carried branches or knives or in one case an ax handle. They nonetheless hefted their various makeshift clubs and got ready for blood. The torches the mob carried cast a flickering light over the whole scene, and it took Josiah a moment to make out Rider's features from that far off. "Stay there, you, and tell us who you are!" Luckily, the light was too chancy for anyone to make out the confusion on Rider's face before he figured out what he was supposed to say.

"Just a passerby, what heard shots coming from the old house here. I think someone's still loose in there!" Josiah heard the message for what it was, and knew his hired thief had somehow gotten loose of the trap that had been set for him and was now fouling up the plan. Beaumont's mind whirled as he tried to figure the best way to play it from here.

No doubt John and whoever he had snuck inside had killed Pox-Scar and Hawk Nose, or those two would have delivered John up for the noose already. That left Josiah with only the mob and Rider, along with himself. If his grandmother was dead, everything could still be worked out. If she was alive, having the mob along would work against him.

What he needed was to be in the house, away from the eyes of the rabble where he could find out exactly what the situation was and kill his grandmother, if she still drew breath, before the mob saw her. The dangerous part of that idea was exposing himself to John, who was no doubt holed up inside the house.

Josiah waved Rider over to where he stood and spoke in low tones,

"We've got to get in there. I'll head around back and go in. I know this house in the dark and can make my way. You keep anyone who's currently in from getting out through windows, doors or otherwise."

The man on the horse nodded once and gripped his reins a bit tighter, finally deciding to speak up. "You never told us there'd be anything like this."

Josiah only shook his head. "Just think, all their shares are yours now."

Beaumont was already headed away so he couldn't hear the man he called Rider's reply, said in a near whisper. "The dead can't spend any amount of money, jackass." As soon as Josiah disappeared around the corner of the house, Rider yanked his horse's head around and rode through mob, who parted before him with shrieks and shouts of anger.

Over his shoulder the last survivor of Beaumont's cutthroats called out, "I'm ridin' to git the law! Ya'll keep anyone from gittin' away!" Behind the manse all Beaumont heard was a ragged cheer from his rabble, and he unwittingly smiled in satisfaction.

The quiet ways around and into the mansion had been known to Josiah since he was a boy, seeking secrecy to carry out his impulses, secrecy to satisfy his needs. Now Beaumont moved once again around the home of his family, no less quiet or secreted than he had been those years ago. When the cheer had come up from in front of the house he imagined his agent, Rider, to have told the crowd of Mr. Beaumont's courage in seeking entrance himself, to better confront the deplorable killers of his family.

He stood in front of the low kitchen window he had so often used. Slowly he checked his pistol in its holster and the derringer in his hat band. His weapons were ready and he took a deep breath before sliding the window slowly and silently open. In front of the house he could hear glass breaking as his lynch mob grew unruly. Josiah froze as two quick rifle reports cracked the sound of the mob into silence. Fired quickly enough signify a repeater, whoever was behind the sight of that rifle knew his business.

Finally, he set his foot onto polished hardwood floor of the kitchen and began to make his way into the house. Into the kitchen of the house that was his birthright. Into *his* house.

# THIRTY EIGHT

Corsey heard the crowd raise a cheer while he was walking towards the back of the house, but couldn't pay it any mind. He was going to have to out fight Beaumont, now, or Lydia, Geraldine and himself would all die. Corsey's problems were that he was wounded, that he had to keep Geraldine alive if he wanted to get out of the fouled-up situation without killing his way through that mob outside, and that there was no way he could keep Josiah out of the house.

Corsey could leave Geraldine to Lydia, and his wounds could be ignored for a time, but Josiah Beaumont was most likely already in the house. Corsey stopped short in the dining room, straining to hear any sound of movement in the house. He stood that way for nearly a minute before a crash of glass followed by Lydia's rifle ruined his hearing.

"That man of yours seems a

225

hard type, my dear." Lydia spared one look at the old matriarch before sighting back down the barrel of her rifle. Geraldine took one step back at that look, how could such a young and comely woman be capable of that stony, cold, snake-eyed stare?

The younger woman replied with words. "Iyaye taŋyaŋ, kuŋśi."[*]

Geraldine's spirit dropped. She turned and shuffled out of the room, not understanding the strange words or demeanor that had fallen over this person she thought she knew, at least a little. She slowly made her way down the stairs, clutching the ornate rail to keep herself balanced. As she took the final step down a voice she hoped never to hear again sounded out in dulcet tones and sweet words that sent a lightning bolt of fear down her back and into her gut.

"Hello, grandmother. It has been some time since our last conversation, non? Yet I still recall how you enjoyed a peppering of the old language when we spoke, 'How it sounds to the ear!'

---

[*]Leave now grandmother, and be well

you would exclaim."

Josiah, her grandson, had come home.

From his place in the dining room, Corsey could hear Beaumont talking. He slowly cocked the hammer on his pistol back. He moved, but his wounded leg flared a bolt of pain that sent him staggering sideways, crashing into a nearby chair, overturning it, and sending it clattering across the floor. Corsey managed to catch himself on the table, but his gun went off. Corsey straightened up and he did it slow, keeping his hands flat on the table and setting his pistol down on the clean linen of the tablecloth.

Josiah Beaumont stood in the doorway, his fancified, silver filigreed pistol in his right hand and his grandmother's arm in his left. A grin of true glee split the noble features of the dandy. Corsey had last seen him in a mud hut back in Texas.

Beaumont spoke, and he knew everything. "Well well well, Mister Fisk. What a pleasant turn. For you to have put the pieces together this quickly is impressive indeed, and so far from anyone you know! Well done! Where are my manners? John, this is my own sweet Grand-dame Miss Geraldine Beaumont, Gran'ma this is an employee of mine known to me alternately as Mister Fisk and John." Corsey stood and waited for a chance to do something. Unless Beaumont made a mistake in the next few minutes John would die in the dining room. Beaumont yanked the old lady's arm and she fell to the floor in front of him, between the two men.

"See how mannerly we are here in the South, Mister Fisk? Have you ever seen a curtsy so low or stately?" he said mockingly.

Geraldine knew about her grandson. She hadn't tried to scream and she forwent any pleading or whimpering to avoid incensing him. As she watched John she saw him waiting, his features drawn and pale with blood loss but also still as stone. He wasn't listening to Josiah, he was waiting for a chance. She let loose with a piteous old woman's wail, and covered her face with her hands as she kept on screaming. It was easier for her to continue after Josiah stepped hard on her ankle and the brittle bones gave way with a small cracking noise. Geraldine knew about her grandson.

Josiah was in full control of the situation and enjoying every second of his victory. He wanted to be sure he could savor it later on in his life, a treasure for his declining years. Then the old woman screamed. He kept the gun steady on John and stomped down on the old biddy's ankle even though he knew it was a bad idea. Even though John was very, very good.

Corsey went for his gun and felt the stitches in his back tear from the exertion. His wounds took their toll, and he was too slow. Beaumont snapped off two shots, the first ripped into Corsey's forearm, and he felt one of the bones there break under the hammer blow of the bullet. The second went wild and plowed into the table, throwing a shower of splinters at him. He held up his fractured right arm to protect his face, forgetting until the pain hit that it was broken. Corsey yelled in pain and nearly blacked out, but kept his feet.

Beaumont was taking his time for the third shot, lining it up real careful.

John knew he was finished.

Josiah aimed down the length of his arm, ready to make an end so he could do right by his grandmother.

The foot on his grandmother was yanked out from under him. He teetered on the edge of falling over, and had to put out his gun hand to the wall to steady himself. He felt claws tearing at his pants and ripping at his flesh. He looked down to see the face of his grandmother, twisted with pain and rage as she attacked him. Josiah laughed and swatted her away with a backhanded swipe.

She seemed to weigh no more than a bundle of sticks and was flung across the room. Red tinged his vision as he started after her, only realizing too late that he had made a terrible mistake.

Corsey forced his mind and his battered body to focus. He reached, even though the motion made blood flow more freely out of his back, and picked up his gun. His vision was starting to gray out at the edges and everything he could see started to waver. Even in this condition he didn't start yanking the trigger, instead he took his time and aimed at Josiah. Corsey squeezed the trigger, and Beaumont fell out of view, his cry of pain, frustration and anger nearly equaled the blast from the gunshot.

Josiah lay on the floor, shot through the chest, a pink froth already starting at the corners of his mouth. Beaumont could still see his gran'ma so he reached for his fallen hat. He felt more than heard John hit the floor behind him, Beaumont had to believe the thief was dead, finally. Josiah's hat lay just out of reach, so he shimmied forward on the floor, groaning each with each movement. Something crashed in through one of the front windows. The crowd was obviously becoming restless. Josiah found he didn't care about the house anymore. All he cared about was putting a bullet through his sweet old granny's face, watching all that glorious destruction unravel her. He had finally gotten close enough to pull the derringer from his hat band when heard something from behind him.

It sounded distinctly like the lever action of a repeater rifle.

Lydia worked the action on her rifle, racking another cartridge into the chamber. Beaumont had a gun: a tiny thing, something a dandy like himself or a white woman would secret on his or her person. Josiah started to point it at her and she bore down on the trigger of the rifle. The .45 caliber bullet took most of the right side of his face and painted it across the floor. Geraldine stirred and moaned a bit, but Lydia did not see John until she came around the dinner table.

She started to work the action again, but dropped the rifle to the hardwood floor with a clatter when she saw John.

She knelt, whispering in his ear. "Iyaye śni. Kitka John kuwa kitka kuwa kitka. Don't leave, wake up John, come here and wake up. Come back, wake up John please we have to go. Kitka John kitka."

A weak grip on her wrist told her that Geraldine Beaumont had come to.

"Child, that isn't going to save him. You have to stop the bleeding and warm him up."

Lydia stopped her whispering and nodded, she set the man down as gently as she could and began to tear the tablecloth into pieces.

Geraldine spoke once again from the floor. "You might do well to call on that mob out there to see if anyone has any experience in doctoring the wounded."

Lydia heard the matriarch spit and when she walked past Josiah's body to get to the door she could see the phlegmy mess running down what was left of his face.

The mob surged forward when the door opened, ready for instant action. What they saw astounded them. A girl, her clothing stained dark nearly everywhere with blood, strode out of the door and stopped them in their tracks. She was pale, with shining black hair that fell straight from her scalp to the middle of her back and she had a wide line of blood streaked under her right eye. Unbelievably, this apparition spoke in human words and not the language of the damned.

"Is there anyone here who knows the binding of wounds and care of the gravely injured?"

# EPILOGUE

The wagon rolled to a stop in the town of Clear Water, Colorado in front of a smoking ruin that had once been Shorty's Hotel. Lydia stared at it without feeling, the man sitting next to her said, "Keep on to the stable."

She got the horse moving again with a quick snap of the reins. After the wagon and animal were seen to, she helped the man walk with her to the Silver River saloon with a steadying hand on his elbow. He brushed it away and gave her bottom a swat.

"No more of that now, I'm healed up enough to walk."

She followed him into the big open door of the bar. They took a table, ordered food and while they waited for it to arrive another man sat down with them. His face was a horror until he smiled.

Revealing what few whole teeth he had left and the jagged splintered remains of the rest made it a tragedy.

He had been beaten badly, recently. He approached the table with a heavy, pronounced limp. Lydia wondered what the poor soul could want from them.

John said, "Sunshine. Hope you got a reason for burning down the hotel."

Roberts spoke through broken lips. "Marshal's after you. Name of Jones, and I had to give up the name of the hotel to keep my left hand intact."

Roberts settled the twisted and useless fingers of his right hand on the table.

Corsey looked on, silent.

Lydia cleared her throat and said, "Jones? Harvey Jones?"

Sunshine nodded and the girl turned away...

# Acknowledgments

I did more revising and more editing on this book than I did on Crow Wing, and I think the quality is much improved. I owe all of that work to my fabulous beta readers. By no means an exhaustive list: Ben Wheeler-Floyd, Josh Johnson, Joel Falensheck, Aron Robison, Julie Abraham, and Phil Sprafka. No man should be so lucky as to have the friends that I do.

I've got to thank me Ma for supporting me unfailingly. Likewise I have to thank my Dad for always asking "Selling any of those books, or what?" To my sister the Bear. Thanks for being there, Carrie Ann.

Here's to everyone out there in the Twitterverse and on the Facebox, turning social media into the best marketing tool I have. Thanks!

Finally, to all of you out there who threw good money after bad and picked up a second book that I wrote, thank you.

Keep an eye out for a short story collection I'm putting together. I think you'll like it. I'm working over ideas for a third book in this line as well.

Lydia, Corsey and Jones will ride again.

*Meet the author!*

Follow Jesse on Twitter under the handle @TheVanDeWriter

LIKE Jesse's author page on FaceBook at www.facebook.com/thevandewriter

Visit Jesse's author spotlight on Lulu www.lulu.com/spotlight/thevandewriter to get his other books